THE
ILLUSTRATOR

THE
ILLUSTRATOR

A NOVEL BY
GERARD BROOKER

Tate Publishing & Enterprises

Published by Tate Publishing & Enterprises, LLC
127 E. Trade Center Terrace | Mustang, Oklahoma 73064 USA
1.888.361.9473 | www.tatepublishing.com

Tate Publishing is committed to excellence in the publishing industry. The company reflects the philosophy established by the founders, based on Psalm 68:11,
"The Lord gave the word and great was the company of those who published it."

Book design copyright © 2008 by Tate Publishing, LLC. All rights reserved.
Cover design by Leah LeFlore
Interior design by Kandi Evans

Published in the United States of America
ISBN: 978-1-60604-030-0
1. Fiction: Historical: General
2. Fiction: War and Military
08.03.19

ACKNOWLEGEMENTS

To Sheila Moore-Brooker for her insights about the possibilities of plot.

To the staff of the Bethel Public Library for their research assistance.

To my writer's group: Lauren Baratz-Logsted, Andrea Schicke Hirsch, Greg Logsted, Robert Mayette, and Lauren Catherine Simpson. Their help is deeply appreciated.

To Cheryl de la Gueronniere for providing me with background advice about Jewish history and culture.

To Holly Shapiro whose way of being sparked in me a deep love for the Jewish people.

To Amy Gaal for her technical assistance.

To Sue Ginter for sharing her sensibilities about imagery with me.

To the founders of the Yad Vashem Children's Museum in Jerusalem. I have rarely been so moved.

To John and Caren Collier for enhancing the historical accuracy of the cover, and Kandi Evans for the creative interior design.

And to the staff at Tate Publishing, extraordinary one and all, especially J.D. Byrum, editor *par excellence,* and Leah LeFlore for the great cover.

You have each given to me the invaluable grace of your assistance. I am grateful for the gifts.

DEDICATION

To the one and a half million children murdered in the
Holocaust.

1.

Some men need evidence to know. Blood on the hands. Ashes in the mouth. Others are gifted with an inner sense of knowing. They live in their hearts which tell them things.

And so Tyszka knew that the stones of their little farm in the village of Oswiecim were witnessing something terrible, a thing so dark that he knew his mind could never comprehend it.

Cecylia had told him the bits and pieces of stories going around about what was happening to Jews across Eastern Europe, the public humiliations, smashed windows, and laws that denigrated her people.

Until he smelled the intensity and volume of smoke increasing in recent weeks, he didn't know the full horror. When he figured it out, he was angry with himself for not knowing sooner.

"Get your clothes on immediately," the kapitan shouted at him. "Commandant Hoss wishes to see you. Gather your art supplies. Be prepared to illustrate."

Tyszka quickly took off his pajamas, put on his winter clothes that consisted of woolen shirt, pants and socks, boots, gray-canvas cap, and a jacket thinly lined with down. He retrieved his kit of art supplies, and forgot his gloves.

"I am ready," he said to the impatient Waffen-SS officer.

Three armed soldiers escorted him to a command car, no doubt Hoss's own, for the short trip into the camp.

The entrance was a site already familiar to Tyszka who often passed it delivering vegetables from his father's tiny farm. Trains and trucks from the nearby Camp Birkenau that brought Jews to this entrance stopped here, mostly in the evening. First at the gate, then they pulled into the camp ever so slowly before the men, women, and children were dumped out like trash from garbage cans.

It was clear to Tyszka that the numbers of Jews being brought in could not be quartered in such a small camp. He created a grammatical problem out of this obvious discrepancy. His teachers had taught him to use the word "fewer" for things that were countable, and the word "less" for those that were not, such as the grains of sand on a beach. Yet he was not certain how he should think about the inconsistency between the number of Jews being brought on cattle cars into the camp and the camp's capacity to hold them. Would he say there are fewer Jews in the barracks than the number he saw going in or, so many that he would say there are less Jews?

This way of looking at things was a turn of mind Tyszka had. It was at once creative in its genesis, while practical in its usefulness, to yield information that would pass by most people. It was a good skill to have in 1944. In Poland, as a neighbor to the Auschwitz concentration camp.

As they pulled up to one of the barracks, two Gestapo officers walked briskly toward the car. Shined boots, smartly capped black uniforms, and pistols that hung in tight holsters on their waists gave them a formidable appearance.

One of the officers took Tyszka by the arm and led him into a foyer, told him to sit, then knocked on the commandant's door. He stared at the door, eventually placing his left wrist behind his back before grasping it with his right hand. He did not change position for five minutes until Commandant Hoss shouted, "Come in."

A woman, young, not pretty yet robust, walked out, crossed the sitting room while staring straight ahead, and exited into the mud-pebbled streets that connected the barracks.

The arm-grabbing officer connected again and Tyszka was escorted into the office.

He knew where he was, yet did not know how to comport himself. The son of a farmer, he had never been in the company of an important person. In some strange way, though, he felt himself to be important today, here in this man's office. He knew that his skills as an illustrator were noted in his little community, that people came to him to have their faces sketched on a pad with pen and ink. Although he was the only one in the area who practiced the craft, he was admired for the level of his skills.

Most folks in the area also looked up to him because he was self-taught. He did not bear the cross of formal education that was at once respected and suspect.

He was frequently asked how he learned to sketch faces with such accuracy. Some said that he could capture the soul of a person on paper. Many young couples brought their first child to him, so that later, when life became hard, they could take out the illustration of the baby's face and remember him when he was still happy.

Tyszka did not like to call himself an artist, even a sketch artist. For him, artists painted in oils or water colors, and sketch artists tried to find the nuances of beauty in their customers. Caricaturists were another thing.

With a faculty that enabled him to see into character and personality, Tyszka could only find the bare soul in his subject, and then he would try to illustrate its spirit as it revealed itself to him.

"So, you are Tyszka Dunajski," the commandant said from behind a large desk that was clean except for a holstered pistol resting at one of the edges. A smaller, working desk, piled with stacks of papers and folders, was located in a corner of the room to the left of the big desk.

"I hear that you are an illustrator, that you sketch people's faces. And that you are good."

"Yes, sir, I sketch people's faces. Mostly at weddings and baptisms."

At this, there was an awkward silence, as if Tyszka's response set off a counter-point reaction in the commandant to the images of joy and babies.

"I want you to sketch me. My face and chest. But I don't want your happy bride and groom stuff. No fat cherub insinuations. I want you to sketch me as I am. I pride accuracy and precision. They guide the way I run this camp. Without them, life is sloppy, awkward, out of hand. Life must be governed by exactness of execution in everything we do. If not, the forces eat us up like wild trees edging themselves into the windows of houses that have been empty for a long time.

"Do you understand me?"

"Yes, Herr Commandant."

Hoss indicated to one of the SS to check Tyszka's supply folder which was made of brown leather, held by belt and clasp. The officer placed each item in turn on the large desk, careful not to touch the holster: charcoal pens, erasers, a small watercolor palette with brushes, several watercolor blocks, a water tin, and two pads of drawing paper.

He turned the open folder upside down and shook it.

"Put your stuff back in," he commanded.

"While you get ready," Hoss said, "I am going to change clothes to my full-dress uniform. I am correct, am I not, that you will depict me from the upper chest and face?"

"That is the usual, Herr Commandant. But, if you wish to have your cap on, I will illustrate you from the neck up. If you insist, I can do it from the chest on up, but the paper I use is standard size, so your face will naturally be smaller."

"Do it from my neck up," Hoss said before hesitating.

"After all, with one exception, that is my best part. Wouldn't you say?"

"Absolutely, sir, your best part."

2.

The outskirts of the village of Oswiecim began and ended in the same place, about three hundred yards from the entrance to Auschwitz, on the Ofiar Faszyzmu road.

Tyszka and his father's small two-story home was the last house at the end of the village, just before the plot of land that separated it from the camp. After an inquisitive old man and his wife were pistol-whipped there by two camp officers the year before, it was understood that no one was allowed to stroll in that area. The townspeople called this section of overgrown grass *niemandsland*.

The two-story Dunajski house was a white-wood and brick structure covered by a V-shaped roof. It had three bedrooms, a kitchen with coal stove for cooking and heating, and a living room. The only window on the long side of the house allowed Tyzka to look out to the end of the railroad tracks that brought Jews from all over Eastern Europe to Auschwitz.

With the Zeiss binoculars his father bought him for his twenty-first birthday, he would peek out the window between a slit in the drawn curtains. Trains of cattle cars, some days by the dozens, pulled up to the gate where civilian and uniformed guards would emerge to drag the occupants out of the wooden cars.

He would often use the wide-angle binoculars to look at the faces of the victims who appeared haggard and confused. How alone and abandoned they seemed. How frightened by the police dogs that were trained to inflict the fear and punishment maliciously ordered by their masters.

One afternoon that summer he witnessed an attack on a young father. He was simply trying to protect his son who appeared afraid of one of the dogs that was aggressively leading its handler toward the boy. Just as the man pulled his frightened son into himself to protect him, the guard in one motion ripped the boy from him while ordering the dog to attack. The large animal tore his teeth into the man's left leg several times, ripping his pants which soon became wet with blood. The boy began to shiver before the guard called off the dog and ordered two kapos to take the man to the infirmary. The boy held onto his father's leg with both of his arms, wanting them to stop the bleeding.

It was an experience that helped transform Tyszka's attitude from horror to shocking disbelief at what was happening. He would have to do something about it. Even as a small boy, he felt a certain rage whenever he saw any of his little friends in school bully another.

The number of prisoners going into the camps and those marching from Birkenau to work at the I.G. Farben factory in Monowitz less than three miles away was disproportionate. It was evident that most of the Jews going into the two camps were being killed, but he didn't know how. Nor did he know where the bodies were being buried.

There was the sweet and sour smell of the smoke that came day and night from the stacks. *Could it be that they were burning the bodies?* He wondered. *But how?*

He was an ordinary man, son of farmers, an illustrator. He could not do much about what he saw, yet he could do something. His mother, dead from a winter bout with Spanish influenza long before the horrors began, was a good and simple peasant who taught her son the ways of goodness. She told him that, although he should always long to be free, that a desire to stop the swagger of the bully was not good enough. He must be terminated. Such was the degree of hatred this sweet lady bore for certain dark ways of man. Simple theft and rape were included.

She also taught her only son that if he could not terminate the evil-doer, he must at least try. To show him what she meant, she took him one day to the pond that was off to one side of the village, in the space where the spotted houses on the outskirts began. She picked up a tiny pebble and placed it in the boy's hand.

"Here, Tyszka, this is what you can do with your life. You are the pebble. You can lie on the ground for your whole life and be downtrodden like Poland so often is. Or you can get up and throw yourself into your life.

"Throw the pebble into the pond, my son."

He did. And he watched it ripple out.

He began his ripple by a most brave act. After talking with Cecylia one entire afternoon about his anger at the dog handler, he decided to do something about it. He couldn't stop the dogs, but he could make a few of the prisoners stronger.

"Cecylia, I am going to go out tonight and under the cover of darkness I will go to the barbed wire fence at the eastern side of the camp and put a bag of vegetables from our plot under it. I will put a note in it to ask if anyone got the bag."

"You stupid man," she blurted out.

He looked up at her from his bed where he was sitting, hurt in his eyes. Since life had become dangerous for Polish Jews, she would often come to his room to sit and talk. She was in no immediate danger because the authorities were trying to keep the routine of Oswiecim as ordinary as possible. Edgy disruptions were not Commandant Hoss's way, although a woman as pretty as Cecylia was always on her guard against over-reacting when Gestapo officers glided a hand across her body below the waist while pretending to pass by her in one of the crowded shops.

Tyszka and Cecylia had been friends since childhood. She was one grade in front of him in school. He was pulled to her with the gravitational naturalness that attracts moons to planets. Even when he chose her from the many playmates in school to throw his snowballs at, he sensed in the smart ways of little boys that she was special. He liked it best when he bombarded her in a flurry of soft snowballs and she would fall down as if wounded, only to laugh full out with the joy of it all when he would bend over her to see if she was all right. Something in him lit up at the sight of her lying there laughing.

It was in his fifteenth year that Tyszka realized he loved her. That was the year her father died suddenly of a heart attack.

Cecylia loved her father. It was easy for someone of her nature to idealize him. Her mother was a woman overcome by a fear that lived in her like so many slim strings of fireworks forever exploding in the pit of her stomach. As a consequence, she could be relied on for very little. And her husband for much.

He worked the chicken farm they owned, small as it was. He sold some of the hens and others they ate, along with the vegetables he grew or for which he bartered. When Cecylia's mother would grow irritable and edgy with one or both of them, he would sit his wife down on the child's sofa bed, rock her in his arms made strong by work, and hum a simple song. Sometimes after this, she would calm down and return to them.

He was stern about Cecylia's chores and her report cards, yet he never yelled when she failed him. At those times he would sit her next to him at the kitchen table he made, fix a glass of his beloved tea, steeped and always ready on the warm stove, and talk with her about the ways that good people, especially family members, relate to each other. How each one relied on the other. That reliance was the difference between families that believed in each other and the ones who were lost. It was very different, he would tell her, to live in a family whose members trusted each other, and in one of those that didn't. He told her that reliance would overcome all obstacles. And she believed him.

Yet, for some time when she was a teenager, she dreaded the evenings when he would pour tea and ask her to sit at the table for another one of his talks. In Tyszka's room that day, she thought about her father.

"Tyszka, I'm sorry I called you a name. I do not think of you that way. But going to the camp tonight is a very dangerous thing. You know what they will do with you if you are caught. You must be responsible to your father and to those who love you."

At that moment, he wanted to ask her if she was one of those who loved him. He was afraid to ask, so he turned to another fear.

"It's not as if I am not scared to do it tonight. I am. But I cannot sit back and do nothing. They are your people. I can see when they enter, the yellow star, the same one you must wear, on their arms.

"When I will help them, I am helping you. Please tell me you understand what I am saying."

He was afraid to say that in loving them he was loving her.

Maybe it was the complete acceptance that while trying to help others tonight he might himself die. Or maybe it was that he couldn't stand the tension of his unspoken love for her that Tyszka blurted out, "Cecylia, I want to ask you to do something for me today, now, before you go."

The request was more sincere and serious than she was used to hearing from him. Mostly, he disguised the depth of his feelings for fear that they might scare her away.

"I still think you're wrong in going out there tonight. If you get caught—" She stopped. Tyszka could see her slightly almond-shaped eyes water. Yet without realizing or intending it, she killed his moment, saying, "You should be responsible to your father and yourself. Nevertheless, what can I do for you?"

He could feel the confidence of the minute before ebbing out of him.

"I have often wanted to ask you this, but I lack the courage to ask, as you might think I am crazy."

In the way that often complicated his attempts to simplify, he said, "I think highly of you. I know I have not yet done much with my life. I mean I don't have a life that a woman would be proud of. But, again, I have a request to make of you."

"Say it, please."

"As I might be killed tonight, I want you to do something for me," and before his weakness could interrupt him, he blurted out, "I want you to breathe into my mouth."

Cecylia hardly knew whether to laugh out loud, as this might be one of Tyszka's jokes, or keep it to herself because he might be serious. She could not always figure him out.

She decided to be safe, to not take the chance that she might hurt his feelings twice in one day.

"Why do you want me to do that?" she asked with a twinkle in her eye that she could not hide from the man she sometimes thought of as her younger brother.

"I have read that if you suck in the breath of another person, then that person's spirit will live in your soul. It is a beautiful idea, one I believe in."

She was touched that he would want her to live in him. In that moment she saw him as other than a brother. With the bang of insight, she understood the warm ways he looked at her, the care he took for her safety since the Germans took over, and the lightness that seemed to seize him whenever they spoke, especially when they hadn't seen each other for a while. Although he always made her feel special, it was not until this moment that she understood why.

"Tyszka, I don't know what to say to you. I don't even remember if I brushed my teeth today."

He startled himself by reaching his hand as if to brush her face. The back of his fingers touched her as if they were lips caressing. The move was gentle and he could feel his skin flirt with the microscopic fuzz on her cheek that could be seen only in a certain afternoon light.

"Cecylia, I might never have what it takes to ask you this again. Please don't make fun of me."

She would never make fun at times like this, as her sense of the moment was true.

"Tyszka, I'd like to do as you ask. But I don't know what I would tell Kryztof. He thinks he is engaged to me."

3.

Except for Cecylia, Tyszka did not tell anyone about his plans for helping some of the prisoners in the camp. For weeks he had hidden a few carrots now and then, as well as some vegetables from the cellar where his father kept them. In this way, the loss would not be noticeable.

He waited until eleven o'clock that night before sneaking across *niemandsland* to a part of the camp where he knew the prisoners gathered for roll call in the mornings and where they came back in the early evening from work at the factory nearby. They were allowed to linger in the same place for a while before being fed a meager soup and a small fistful of bread baked with straw in it. It was a good place for prisoners to spot a brown bag stuffed under the barbed wire, especially before the camp guards began to assemble at 6:30 in the morning for their work-party duties which consisted of taking the roll, marching prisoners to the factory, supervising the work, and then guarding the prisoners on their way back to the camp.

He had watched the night-time routine of the guards in the watchtowers. There were always two of them in each tower. One would be ready with his rifle, while the other kept control of the search lights. They used the lights mainly to illuminate the muddy paths that connected the red-bricked barracks that were now being used to house the prisoners. About every five minutes they would cast the lights on "No Man's Land."

All he had to do, he thought, was to run across the open space during those five-minute intervals, ball himself up in the high grass near the wire, then dash to the fence, dig fast to put the food bag under and across the wire to the other side, run back to the tall grass, and wait until the next survey of light was over. Then he could run all the way back to his house.

The first time he tried, he executed his plan with impeccable timing, aided by good luck. When he fell down in a wet spot on his way back to the tall grass, his right foot grabbed hold of a hard patch allowing his momentum to push him straight up for the mad dash back to safety.

These are for you, the note read. *Please take them from us as a gift.*

We want you to know that some of us out here are thinking of you.

If you want more, tuck this samebag almost fully in the mud in the

exact spot. In one week we will bring more. Unless the moon is bright.

Tyszka's naivete was not without limits. He did not sign the note.

4.

"The commandant wants to see you immediately. Put on your clothes and gather your supplies. Be ready in five minutes."

The periodic summones were inflexible in routine. They usually started at midnight with a pounding on his door, followed by barked orders and a silent ride to Commandant Hoss's office.

The regularity of the late night calls not only interfered with Tyszka's sleep. It also got in the way of his artistic integrity.

For several weeks now, he had violated the natural truth of his art. He could only illustrate the bare soul of whomever he depicted with charcoal. But, he was lying to himself and to his craft when he drew Hoss.

At first, Tyszka's hand could hardly move his charcoal pen across the paper. He asked the commandant to sit straight up in a simple wooden chair, in front of a bare wall, the best way, he explained, to avoid background distractions. Hoss immediately ordered the wall to be stripped of any hangings, and had it painted a soft cream.

He always followed the same routine for sittings. As soon as he was ready, he would have Tyszka brought into his office. He would stand up behind his desk, reach his hand out to welcome the illustrator, sit back down, open a large narrow drawer in the middle of his desk, and take out the drawing from the previous session.

Even the inevitable critique that followed was along uniform lines.

"The peak of the cap is too high. Measure it exactly the next time so that it is in perfect proportion to the rest of its measurements.

"The eyes are too narrow." He would grow agitated. "See mine, look here, look into my eyes. See, you see! They are not narrow. They are open. Open to life, open to the world."

At times like this, he would stop and move right up into Tyszka's face and say with blazing eyes, "Get them right the next time."

Tyszka knew that if he got them right by the commandant that he would not be accurate, could not let the antennas that informed his gift to tune into the subject's character and personality. If he did, the commandant would not like it, and the consequences could be fatal.

At these times, Tyszka would think about Cecylia's reprimand to him about responsibility to his father and to those who loved him.

He was being forced to portray ugliness as elegant, an ill-proportioned soul as balanced.

Until Hoss came along, the work had always been joyful for him. The souls of baptized babies were always good and pure. After feeding at their mother's breasts, they even beamed, lacking nothing.

For some time, though, he had battled within himself whether to illustrate babies only after they had been christened. According to the doctrine of his church, before the sign of God was inscribed in holy oil on their foreheads, and cleansing waters poured over their almost hairless heads, they were said to be impure, not worthy to be in the sight of God.

If they should die before being baptized, they would be relegated to a place called Limbo where they would live for eternity without ever being allowed to know the giddiness of being in the holy presence.

The doctrine troubled Tyszka. So, he decided one day to allow his gift to calibrate the accuracy of his insight. He asked one of the new mothers in the village if he could illustrate her baby boy the day before as well as the day of his baptism, explaining to her that he wanted only to practice once before he did the special illustration.

What he really wanted to know was not so much about the holiness of the babies before or after baptism. He had already decided that matter for himself. In their innocence, they were always holy, pure, and beautiful. Before or after baptism. They could not be less. If chance or random phenomena happened before the ritual, such as a sudden flood bloating and bleaching their bodies, or a nighttime of twisting and turning that might smother them in their tiny blankets, most certainly the transcendent power would embrace them.

"Please come to our house on Saturday," Mrs. Gadzal told him. "We will have the baby clothed in his baptismal dress, the same one that I used, the same one my mother used. Please practice on him for the real drawing the next day after church."

He did as he was told. When he got to the Gadzal house, the baby was already fed and clothed in the cloth of antiquity. Tyszka asked the mother to prop the baby up on pillows so he could see his little face.

Tyszka was ready. His fingers, charcoal pen in hand, trembled with the gift. Left to its nature, his hand could not quibble with the truth. It would draw only what Tyszka's sixth sense about people told it to draw, nothing more, nothing less. If the baby was as the teachings of his church told him, the clairvoyant hand of the illustrator would find a spirit unworthy to stand before the throne of God. Tyzka needed to know if his art coincided with his beliefs.

Would his brush connect the child's lip and cheek in a way that reflected his potential for human compassion? Would the baby's eyes sparkle with the light of love? Would the parts come together, each complementing the other, to create a compassionate countenance?

Tyszka sketched the baby's face with as much mind-fulness as he could without drawing outside the margin where his intuitions lived. Being too careful or not cautious enough was like throwing dirt into a fragile mechanism. Excess in either direction would cause him to miss the truth of his subject, the truth of his art.

Although it was nearly winter in the house heated slightly by a small coal-burning stove, he was sweating when he finished after a half hour. Tyszka thought about how Jesus, wanting so much to be true to his father's calling, sweated blood in the garden of Gethsemane the night before he died.

He had done his best, yet needed to have the results confirmed. Today, the illustrator did not know how to judge his work. Sometimes, the difference between the depiction of righteousness and wickedness was so subtle that it was hard to tell the difference. Is the hint around the lips a smile or a sneer? The beam in the eye a gleam of love or a suggestion of hate?

Tyszka's heart was knotted with many problems. Perhaps too many to bear while trying to keep his craft pure. Maybe the baby was unclean, yet he could not perceive that anymore, now that he was being deceitful in depicting Commandant Hoss. *For all I know*, he thought, *compromise may be killing the gift.*

Suddenly, he was not sure anymore if he even had a gift.

"Here, Mrs. Gadzal. Your baby Bazyli. What do you think?"

She took the drawing paper and stared intensely at it for a moment, without realizing that she was being given the authority to judge the accuracy of Tyszka's art as well as the truth of his beliefs.

"You have made my Bazyli as beautiful on this piece of paper as he lies before me."

Her choice of words, intended to convey pleasure at the work done, confused Tyszka more than ever about his gift to convey truth. Could it be that even a child is able to lie? Did her response mean that the deceptions Tyszka had been making in drawing Commandant Hoss had left him no longer able to see into the inner soul of a subject? Perhaps his own artistic lying had corrupted his talent, had unhinged him from his ability to behold truth.

The illustrator was so disturbed by her words that he gathered his supplies and quickly left the house, remembering only the words, "See you tomorrow."

5.

Bazyli was baptized the following day at St. Stanislaus church in a small and quiet ceremony, as it was good not to bring any attention or public notice to oneself in Oswiecim.

A handful of guests, including Cecylia at Tyszka's request, was invited to the Gadzals' house. There was a little wine and several cheeses, but most of the talk lacked the spontaneity and hopefulness of the occasion when, in normal times, hosts and guests would share their joy for the child who was now cleansed from the Original Sin and brought into the fold of God.

Today, the talk was more cautious.

"Father Celmer, I know you have just baptized little Bazyli, but please bless him once again here in our house. And ask the God of our fathers to surround him with love. That he may be loved the way we in this room love him today."

"Mr. Gadzal, I couldn't have said it any better than you have just now. It is a beautiful prayer.

"But I will, as your priest, say a prayer over the little one."

Placing the baby in the crook of his arm, Father Celmer looked into his tiny face and whispered, more to the baby than the elders, "God of the universe, please hold Bazyli in your hands and surround him with the power of your love. I ask this in the name of Jesus, your son."

The silence that followed was punctuated by applause more like a whimper than a bang.

Regina Gadzal took her baby back from the priest and went to her husband's side as the tiny group stood in a circle surrounding them. If only they each could have dispensed the good will that was in the cold farmhouse this day, or clutch the flickering candles to guide their paths.

Cecylia could feel the quiet melancholy in the room, and, as if requesting permission to speak, she said to no one in particular, "What a beautiful baby!"

And the subdued festivities began. Toasts with wine in delicate goblets three generations old. Home-cooked delicacies for the parents, knitted sweaters and booties for Bazyli.

On this day, though, no one spoke a word about the camp the Nazis called Birkenau. Nor about the where-abouts of the vast number of Jews coming out of the cattle cars at Auschwitz or the constant belching of smoke from the stacks, or the slight white coating that was building up on their rooftops. The Gadzals' household was receiving the gift of God's presence renewed in Bazyli on this day. The attendance of his gray-haired grandparents, each honorable by their long commitment to work and family, also made this a day to mark with the stamp of spiritual renewal. If their prayers for the defeat of Germany were not being answered, they could, on this day at least, not talk about them. In that way, at least, they would try to keep their presence out of the room.

Of course, Tyszka, like anyone in love, knew immediately that Cecylia was in the room. He had begun to notice the past few months that whenever she came into a room that she lit it up. As if she was a light, or a presence that glowed light. At first, he thought that he was imagining it. He knew enough about the symptoms of falling in love, how infatuation takes form. But this was real. A sort of mellow glow that quickened to brightness if he continued to look at her.

He had always thought of beauty as light. Sometimes, at bedtime on a day when goodness seemed to surround him, he would lie waiting for sleep to come, thinking that if God were now looking down on the planet, he would see this place, this village, emanating a light so intense that perhaps He, too, might be compelled to join Tyszka in tears of joy.

Aware of Cecylia's presence, he looked up to see her standing next to a well-dressed man who had both hands nestled, one around her hip bone, the other around a glass of wine.

"Tyszka, you remember Kryztof, don't you?"

He looked up from the cribbed baby who also seemed to be bathed in a kind of shining that confused the illustrator who was about to sketch him for the second time.

"Yes, of course," he responded before standing up to shake his hand. "It's good to see you again," he lied.

Kryztof was ten years older than Tyszka. It had taken him one year longer than usual to graduate from dental school in Warsaw before he decided to take up a general practice in Oswiecim two years ago rather than go through a more thorough training in dental surgery, his first interest. Everyone in the area knew his father, a prominent, yet odd, businessman who specialized in developing management teams to oversee the outlets that sold agricultural machinery so vital to the region. He named his son Yehudah, but in place of a traditional Yiddish additional name, he called him Kryztof, a way, he thought, to let his mostly Catholic clients know that he held them in high regard. Kryztof liked the name and when he reached his adulthood, he made it a point to ask, even demand, that everyone call him by it. It was also becoming advantageous.

The new doctor became an instant celebrity among the people he served, though not by way of a code of conduct approved by Tyszka. At once full of life and originality, Dr. Kryztof Penkalski brought new ways to the practice of small-town dentistry. Whenever a youngster was escorted to his office for a visit, he would ask about the child's siblings while currying favor with the parents with candies for the children at home. He treated some patients for free, yet he always asked them not to tell others what he had done.

When Tyszka first heard of this, he concluded the worst about the doctor's insistence on secrecy, interpreting it as a manipulative gesture calculated to achieve the opposite results.

What really made the dentist unworthy in his eyes occurred when he bought uniforms for the young boys' soccer team which then called itself "Kryztof's Kids." This was self-service hiding under the guise of generosity, thought the illustrator who, by this time, had little doubt that were he to portray the dentist on paper, the results would horrify Cecylia.

The dentist did not care about what Tyszka thought of him. His was just another opinion, the way that life was. One would always be liked by some and not by others.

The simple reason he cared whenever Cecylia mentioned Tyszka was the clarity of regard she had for a childhood playmate. She always spoke his name with respect and affection. It would be in the doctor's best interests to win over her friends, especially one whom she held in such esteem.

"Cecylia tells me that you are an excellent illustrator, that you specialize in people's faces. Perhaps one day you will do mine," he said ingratiatingly, or so Tyszka thought.

"Perhaps," Tyszka replied sharply. Realizing immediately that he was being curt, he responded in a tone more fitting to the niceties of the day and in line with his own desire to please Cecylia.

"I must go to work now with the baby. The Gadzols have commissioned me to draw the child."

He amused himself by using the word "commissioned" which represented to him everything that was stuffy about the world of art, as well as some artists who strutted in that world.

"Before I go, may I see you for a minute, Cecylia?"

Before going to him, she squeezed the dentist's hand, a signal that annoyed Tyszka by the implicit intimacy of the act.

Guiding her into a small space of privacy in the crowded room, Tyszka told her that he was especially anxious today. That he needed help delivering food packages to the inmates.

He went on, his nervousness revealed in a staccato rush of personal revelations.

"I illustrated Bazyli yesterday, and I am not sure if I have my gift anymore. I cannot gather enough food for the packages. I don't know if I can continue without getting caught."

His art had always intrigued her and she believed in it, and in him. He knew this. The times when they talked about his ability to depict the central nature of another were the moments he felt closest to her and, he thought, she to him. At the very least, he felt she was paying attention to the uniqueness of the way he signed his signature in life, that she could hear the story of him. Her willingness to do this made him feel loved.

"Tyszka, calm down. It will be OK." It annoyed him when she took the fingers of his left hand with her own in her thoughtful way. Hadn't she just been holding Kryztof"s hand tightly? If the tightness of hand-holding was a sign of her love, then perhaps she felt for him only the affection of a caring woman.

"I can help you with the vegetables. And maybe the other things you mentioned, but this is not a good time."

Whenever she looked at him the way she did now, he felt the light. A light sometimes so intense that Tyszka thought the energy that gave her life must be concentrated in her face where it shined from her eyes. He wanted to open his folder so he could draw her beautiful face and, in this compelling moment, capture by a special stroke, an illusive dab, the pupils of her eyes where the nature of her winsome spirit leaked through to pierce his loneliness.

"I will come to your room in the morning, and we can talk about these things. For now, why don't you sketch baby Bazyli. His parents are waiting for you."

The flow of hopefulness he felt whenever he talked with her ebbed as he watched her go back to the dentist. But he must not put off any further his responsibility to depict the baptized child.

"Mrs. Gadzal, I am ready to illustrate your baby. May we start?"

"Certainly, Tyszka. Wos and I have been waiting."

Again, the baby was propped up on a pillow. And Tyszka worked. The task was an easy one, as his subject had just sucked at the dripping nipples of his mother's love. The only tension in the work came from the illustrator's uncertainty about the effort of the day before.

He had simply taken a peek at the drawing before running home, so frightened was he about the accuracy of his art now that it was being compromised by deceits in sketching the commandant of Birkenau.

Tyszka felt safe in the next half hour as he sketched. No matter the doubts about his continuing ability to retain the extraordinary aesthetic sensibility that was his, today's work was without challenge. "If Bazyli has a soul, it must be beautiful today," he told himself.

Certainly, Bazyli's small body was beautiful. Radiant skin, soft and fresh. Ears like perfect seashells ready to receive the sound of his mother's voice. A nub-cute nose, and eyes that spoke about the excitement of being alive.

Tyszka was always struck with wonder at how disproportionate a baby's skull was to the rest of its head. So large was Bazyli's that his bright eyes were located less than halfway up his face.

As if we must be reminded by a baby of our imperfections, there was a tiny knot, a little skin-ball, showing at the edge of his left ear.

Now that the illustrator saw the fullness of his subject's face, he simply allowed his artistic hand to follow the instructions of his intuitions, and his talent took over. Without effort, his pen pushed the charcoal here, then there. It was as if it had its own mind. A full dab, another less full. One with a broad stroke, the next thin. Wavy, straight. Light, heavy.

Without effort, the strokes connected to each other with the subtle simplicity of the master's moves. Here now was the truth of Bazyli's essential excitement at being alive, a soul's substance transferred to paper.

"Come, Mr. and Mrs. Gadzal, and see your son."

Everyone in the room followed to look. Together, they praised Tyszka, then the baby. Then the Gadzals for birthing Bazyli and having the illustrator here today.

"What do you think?" he asked.

Tyszka grew anxious as they assessed his work. If they found today's results authentically Bazyli and yesterday's but an ugly representation, he could only conclude that the gift was gone. For he was certain that the souls of babies are beautiful, always.

Such a finding, too, would alter, if not destroy, his idea of God as a personal power who loves without conditions, and is without neediness. Tyszka could live with that, but not without his gift.

But what if, he thought, *babies are unworthy before baptism, and yesterday's sketch shows an ugly Bazyli? Would it mean that my gift is intact, that my ability to illustrate the essence of a subject has not been compromised? But that I am wrong about God?*

And if yesterday's and today's babies are both beautiful . . .

His confusion mounted so that he nearly fainted from the pressure. The need for truth about himself, though, was great, and he held on.

6.

Speaking with Cecylia was always the best antidote for Tyszka's confusion.

"You see, the Gadzals and everyone else at the party thought that both of your baby Bazyli's drawings brought out the wonderful glow of innocence in the child. He is beautiful in both of your interpretations," she told him.

"But you don't understand, Cecylia. I do not interpret the spirit of another in my work. I merely portray it as it is."

She lowered her head slightly, a nod of assent to his thoughts, as if she understood.

"I must tell you a secret, Cecylia. For a while now I have been asked by the commandant of the Auschwitz camp to illustrate his face. I think for no other reason than that he is vain and likes to look at himself, as if in a mirror."

Cecylia put her hand to her mouth as if she did not know what to say about this news.

"I didn't know. Why have you not told me?"

"Not to worry you," he responded.

As if comforting herself, she hugged her shoulders with both of her hands.

"It seems like such an awful place. I hear stories. I see things," she said.

"The stories are true, Cecylia. It is an awful place. You know that it is where they take Jews. I am trying to find out more. But I know, I can see with my binoculars from this window, that many come here on trains. Many. And no one, except for the ones who walk to the machine plant, ever leave."

They both knew. Yet, in that strange way that awful truths are sometimes denied, they did not talk about it any further that day.

"I don't know how many times I can violate myself when I illustrate Commandant Hoss. Whenever I begin to sketch him, my right hand works in a fury, as if to get it over with. The pen moves in fits and starts, and it makes edgy strokes. This is when I begin to see the beginnings of evil in his soul. That he is an evil man starts to come through. It is as if I am an instrument of an energy in me that moves the pen in my hands.

"I don't know what to do at these times, except to lie to myself. I do this by imagining an overlay, a mask on his face, one that is good and kind. I mostly try to put discipline into the face because that is what he likes about himself, that he keeps the rules he has established for his own conduct and for the camp, that he is efficient.

"If I sketch him as he truly is, I don't know what might happen to me."

"Tyszka, my poor Tyszka," she replied. "You must not draw him as he is. For your sake, and for those you love, just play with your skill. Put the deceitful mask over him. You must allow the mask to grow more beautiful each time. Increase the wonder of him in his own mind. Do this a little at a time. In this way, you can keep him happy, and he will continue to call on you.

"Never, Tyszka, never illustrate him so he can see himself as perfect. Never. If you allow the completion of whatever in him he is most proud of to come through on paper, he will not need you again. His face will hang on an office wall in an expensive frame, gilded, perhaps. Your name will be on the picture, though you most probably will be dead."

"I never thought of that."

Before he could take a breath, Cecylia asked him to stop putting discipline into Hoss's face.

"Always leave that part just short of coming through. If he misses the point, let him know that you are dissatisfied, that you are trying to put your fingers on some fine point about his efficiency that is missing.

"You have said that he is vain. Nurture his vanity. Make him aspire to some sort of greatness that you will try to capture on paper. You must use your imagination in dealing with him. You are walking on dangerous ground, Tyszka, and I don't want to see you fall."

Saying this, she stepped closer to him, and reached her hand to his face. For a moment, he thought that he felt her love, such was his capacity to yearn.

He quickly broke the tension by sewing new threads on an old conversation.

"When I drew baby Bazyli last Saturday, he had not yet been baptized. Perhaps that is why his right eye in the illustration is a little strange. His left eye seems peaceful and even happy."

"What do you mean, a little strange?"

"The right eye seems frightened, as if it has seen or is about to see something terrible, something incomprehensible to his little mind."

"Or," she interrupted, "something terrible in *your* mind. Perhaps what you see is the speck in his eye that you Catholics talk about. Maybe it is true that the speck is you, your own fears, and not any imperfection in the baby."

"Maybe that is so," he answered.

It might seem strange that someone whose intuitions were as finely tuned as Tyszka's could receive this comment as an epiphany. Yet that was precisely how he heard it. That his artistic sense of another might not be totally pure, that it might be dirtied to some extent by his own clutter. It was as if someone who thought of himself as always being right was finding out that sometimes he was wrong.

He would need time to think about it.

"Cecylia, I need your help to make up bags of vegetables for the prisoners. I cannot continue to steal from my father."

"I told you I would help. What do you need?"

"Lately, I've been sneaking over to the camp about every two weeks. If you could just get me enough food for my next two trips. I will be going again one night from tonight."

She agreed to bring him some carrots and a few potatoes on the following day, the batch after that when it was time.

"I don't know if I can continue doing this without getting caught. I need help."

"I will help you, Tyszka."

"No, no, I will not have your help. It is too dangerous, and you are Jewish!" he blurted out.

He stopped for a moment, sorry that he had yelled this at her.

"Let us stop pretending, Cecylia. We are living in a dream world. We know what is happening. We are but a sliver from the truth of it all. It is only the horror that we do not know. The rest we know."

"It is why I must help you," she repeated.

"No…No! I could not bear the guilt if you got caught. I could not allow myself to ever think of you again."

The words that next came out of Tyszka's mouth were as unexpected as was his boldness in saying them.

"And I would not want to live in a world without you."

Cecylia blushed, yet did not know what to say, an unusual occurrence.

"You must let me help you, Tyszka."

Here it was. An opening for him to express with some clarity the confusing and disconnected thoughts that lately were frequently distracting him. He was not ready to say these things to her, and simply blurted out, "Let Kryztof help me."

"Don't be silly, Tyszka. He is a dentist. He knows how to help others when their teeth hurt. He knows how to help children organize themselves. He knows how to give out candy, to make the little ones happy for a moment. What he does not know is how to be a rebel."

"At least ask him. If not for me, then for your people."

"Tyszka, you know that he is maybe my boyfriend, that he would do this if I asked him. I would then be putting him in danger, the same way that you said you would be doing that to me if I helped you."

"So here we are," Tyszka said, "no one helping anyone because we are all afraid of something happening to someone we—" He stopped, not wanting to say the word. If he did, she would know how deeply he felt about her, and this was not the time. And if he said out loud that Cecylia might love Kryztof, she could be tempted to reveal herself about the dentist, something Tyszka might not want to hear.

Either way, Tyszka thought he would lose. If she admitted that she was in love with the dentist, a last ray of hope in an otherwise dreary world would be extinguished. If she hesitated about such an admission, his hope for her would be reignited. Either was not a good place for him to be during these urgent times.

His decision to get Kryztof involved was at first a practical matter, simply that he needed help in sneaking the food bags under the fence. But at this moment, his request took on another dimension, one that shamed Tyszka.

If Kryztof helped and was caught in the act, he would be imprisoned, perhaps executed. He would be just another Jew in an almost infinite line of Jews pulled to their deaths.

There was a strong chance that this would happen. It bothered Tyszka. Normally, his desire for moral perfection, a desire bordering on compulsion, would not allow him to entertain such a thought, much less be the cause for it to happen.

Once he realized that he would be happy if something bad happened to Kryztof, he decided to take back his request.

"Never mind, Cecylia. You are right. He is not a rebel, nor is he inclined to do more than hand out free candy to children." His sarcasm spoke without his permission.

"You will see, Tyszka, he is a better man than that," she responded abruptly to the barb. "I will ask him tonight."

Fatigued by the recent challenge to his dark side, Tyszka replied, "You are right."

7.

Of course, Kryztof agreed. Perhaps it was his ego or his desire to help. Maybe it was the growing uneasiness he felt concerning Cecylia's recent edginess with him. Or that she was spending more time lately in the bedroom of her childhood friend.

He did not confront her about this or even ask her about it, as he knew she despised jealousy in a man. She referred to any expression of it as coming from "the little boy in the man."

What the little boy did not know was the extent and degree Cecylia was sharing her thoughts with Tyszka about the danger of living in Oswiecim. She was willing to express her fears with him, and free to share how sometimes she thought of herself as being odd. Tyszka did not live in the image others had of him and that freed her to be herself when she was with him. It was difficult to express her likes and dislikes with a jealous man who might not be capable of hearing them with the mature indifference that marked Tyszka most of the time.

"Thank you, Kryztof, for helping. I think it is a better idea if you go with me tonight only a part of the way. I want you to stay by my side until we reach the tall grass. As soon as the searchlight passes over, I will make a run for the fence. You stay in the grass and watch. Watch especially my timing. There is but a five minute interval before the lights will search *niemandsland*. Everything must be done in that span of time. Running to the fence, digging under it, putting the food on the other side, picking up the used bag, and looking for a message. It usually is in the bag from the last delivery. Then I must run back to the tall weeds before the lights again sweep the area. Do you understand?"

"Yes. What time do we meet?"

"Be here at my house at 10:30 tonight. Wear dark clothes, let your beard grow."

"Before I leave you, Tyszka, I have a question. What do they say in the notes they leave?"

"They mostly say thank you, that they are happy that someone out here knows. That the vegetables we leave break the hunger and loneliness that often comes over them. They say they are happy that someone cares. This is what they say."

"I will see you at 10:30. If you need me, I will be at my office or with Cecylia at her house."

As he walked toward Cecylia's, Kryztof knew with an urgency greater than ever before what it meant to be a Jew in Poland on a winter day in 1944. He was nervous about tonight, which made him singularly aware of the yellow star on his arm. He was disheartened that he was no longer able to look away from what he had learned at the professional meetings in Krakow and Poznan, and what he heard in the village, that Jews of every class were being rounded up for trips to work camps, that some were being executed. And that he was one of *them*.

"Cecylia, you know that I must go with Tyszka tonight. I know that he does not think well of me and the ways I go about my business. I know how he looks at me. I know that every time you are with him I can feel you go further away from me, as if what he is saying about me makes you grow indifferent to me."

"It is not true that he says bad things about you. He never speaks about you. That is the truth." She was growing tired of such talk.

"Then, what do you talk about so much?" The wall of reluctance to speak his mind about their relationship was beginning to crack under the urgency of tonight's claim on him. "You spend much time with him. I do not know what you do together."

"If you think we do that, you know—*that*—you are wrong. I have told you I would never do it until I was married by the Rabbi in the synagogue."

"Yes. I know. But, I am tired of playing around the edges of my desire for you." He could not restrain his growing anger at her rejections. "We hold hands, and we kiss sometimes, lightly. Yet, we are hardly ever alone to know each other."

He didn't know how far he wanted to go with this. Quickly, though, he found the insistence of his need thrumming in his loins and rising in his voice.

"Cecylia, tonight I am going with Tyszka to the fence at the camp. It could mean trouble for me. You know that I could be taken away. To the camp. I am a Jew. It could be dangerous. Before I go, please, let us be together in a special way."

He waited, hoping that she understood what he was trying to say.

She came closer to him. "Kryztof, I know we are all scared. Sometimes, I want to make it all go away. I would like to stop thinking about you, about Tyszka, my mother, the Nazis and what they are doing to us." Her lips began to quiver. "I wish I could just let myself be with you in your bed, to make it all go away for a little while, at least. But, I think about Tyszka more each day, and I will not be unaccountable." She paused, trying to feel more resolute than she actually was.

"Kryztof, I will stay in my house tonight while you are going to the fence. I will pray that you and Tyszka are safely delivered. I will think of you, and I will wait to see you tomorrow."

She held out her hand to him. He reached back, and she cupped his hand with both of hers. Friendship, though, would not deliver intimacy today.

8.

If the consumption of vodka could make a gloomy day sunny, Oswiecim would on that day have been warmed over by Kryztof's frequent trips to the cupboard.

Instead, the day was a typical one for December, light without sunshine, air without warmth. In the sullen ways of winter, the day began to shut down by four o'clock, its dim light leaving behind a melancholy ready to drip like slow rain on the dentist's spirit.

By this time he realized that he must stop drinking if he was to be ready for tonight. He drank because he thought it gave direction to his confusion. Yet, on this day confusion reigned.

He wasn't even certain why he had set out to help Tyszka, though the decision seemed to distill the truth of his life into an unpleasant awareness of its shrunken dreams and lost opportunities.

Though not aristocratic, his family, like other Jewish families in Eastern Europe, was learned and possessed the means to send their only son to schools that would eventually allow him to practice a profession, perhaps in Krakow or Warsaw. Following in his father's steps, he would make a contribution to society, and settle into a secure life of leisure accompanied by culture. He would have married within the select circle of influential families, been a dental surgeon to its members, stood tall at dinner parties, drink in hand, telling all who might listen about his children while basking in the beauty of his wife, so charming that other men vied to dance with her. He liked the thought of later at home when they would both laugh at those silly men before making love. Kryztof, of course, the suitor certified by marriage as the most wonderful of all.

It was not to be. The clouds of doom hung over Poland where cities were held in the racist sieges of pogroms and ghettos. It was safer for him to come back to his village, ironically now a locus of the evil he would try tonight to lessen with the presence of his own goodness.

Kryztof realized fully today something about himself that he had never before admitted at the highest levels of his enlightened self. That he cared only about surviving tonight, that he was scared.

"Here, put some of this soot on your face. As soon as we are ready, we will wait until the searchlights go away from the tall grass. I will check my watch, then we will run as fast as we can to hide in the grass. Remember, when the five-minute interval is up, they will shine the lights on the weeds again. As soon as they sweep the lights away from us, I will run to the fence, and you will stay in the grass. You are not to come out of the grass until I get back to you."

He paused to let the instructions sink in again.

"Do you understand?"

"Yes."

"Any questions?"

"No."

"Then, let's go."

Before Kryztof knew what happened, they were in the tall grass of *Niemandsland*. His breathing seemed to be held back by something, as if some sort of gauze was lining the sacks of his lungs. At first, there was a strange stillness in his inner skin. Suddenly, the calm was filled with eerie shouts inside himself, followed by the soft moans of his own dread. It was as if synchronized tuning forks of fear were echoing from his flesh to the barbed-wire fence and back to him again. He wanted to run, but Tyszka was holding his arm.

"Stay here. I'll be right back," Tyszka whispered before he ran to the fence where he reached his hand into the now worn hole and out under the other side. As usual, the last bag, empty now except for a note, was hidden there in the dirt. He quickly covered most of the new bag of food with wet, rocky soil before hunching down while waiting for the path back to be clear of the criss-crossing fingers of light.

Clutching the note in his right hand, the bag in his left, he waited, like a sprinter anticipating the bang of a starter's pistol. As soon as the light left the open field, he lurched out of the starter's block. And just as quickly, he fell in the mud.

Alone, he would have survived by just lying in the mud for the fraction of time required to restore stillness to the scene. He would have known when to get up again, as his intuitions had always served him well.

When he looked up, though, he saw Kryztof running to help him. The movement of the dentist's body, almost flailing in the mud, threw bits and pieces of rocks speckled with quartz into the air, enough to reflect light from a half moon. Just as he reached the fallen illustrator, the tower lights, busy scurrying in the spaces between barracks inside the camp, spun quickly upon them.

Tyszka was angry at the dentist for disobeying his directives. He cursed the night, then the day he might never see again, before getting up to run for home. At the same time, horns began to emit shrill sounds, regular and screechy, confusing Kryztof who suddenly found himself alone in the spotlight. Rifle shots from the nearest tower sprayed around him. The chance he thought he had, though, evaporated once machine gun bullets started to splatter near him, first in a wide circle that slowly grew tighter until he was in a noose of bullets that could choke the life from him.

All of his senses seemed to condense into one he had never before experienced as a total frame of reference. Sights, sounds, taste, touch, smells, each of them became only movement.

The tower beams swirled in a slow cone of light above him, so that each time he tried to look up from the mud he could see only the intense pinpoint of an ophthalmologist's penlight in his eye.

The staccato of .38 caliber machine gun bullets drew a slow-motion necklace around him as they hit the ground, proscribing a new space, tiny and dangerous, in which to stay alive.

He could feel the fear in his mouth move along the edges of his tongue before filling it up with the taste of dry bitter metal.

Kryztof had known terror before. When he was seven. At Zygmunta Street in Krakow when his father, in a drunken rage over a failed business deal, held him by his ankles and hung him out the fourth story window.

See, how do you like that? How does that make you feel? He dangled like a ragdoll, from one ankle, then the other.

As fast as the center of his sentient self became movement, it changed to sound. The machine gun bullets surrounding him bit into the ground with thuds of noise, at first resembling the clinking of wooden sticks which turned to hammers banging on thin metal fences that turned to a rush of raucous horns blasting into his ears.

I could drop you on your head like a rock. All he could express was a chain of noises, linked more by babble than words. Only the good will of his father stood between life and death.

If he had been dropped on his head that day long ago, he would have been killed quickly by the speed of his own weight falling. It would have been over quickly. Waiting for a bullet to crash into his brain tonight, though, seemed to last a long time. Lights, noises, German guards shouting commands and threats he knew well. In reality, perhaps only thirty seconds went by before they were upon him, motioning for him to get up.

9.

Tyszka knocked with an insistence that frightened Cecylia. She was waiting up to hear from Kryztof about his adventures of the night.

"Open the door, open up," was the intense whisper in the night.

He stood there, full of guilt and remorse at what might have happened to the dentist. He couldn't tell if the look on Cecylia's face meant she thought he was Kryztof, or that she was glad to see her dear friend.

In either case, there he was, muddy and shivering, the coldness of the night magnified by fright.

"Come in," she said as she pulled him by his arm.

"What happened?" He seemed to be struck dumb. And she knew.

"Where is Kryztof?"

No answer.

"Tyszka," she repeated, "where is Kryztof?"

"I don't know."

His shivering was getting worse.

"Let me make you some hot tea."

She poured water from a kettle on the stove through the tea filter, then into a glass for him.

"Drink some of this. It'll warm you up."

He did as she asked.

"Everything went according to plan, then I fell. Getting back to the tall grass. I would have been all right. The search lights were going the other way. I could have just gotten up and ran."

"Where is he?" she repeated. "Tell me now, before you tell me the rest!"

"I don't know. He ran to help me, and then the lights came back. There was rifle fire, then machine guns. I just kept on running until I reached the village. I've been hiding for an hour in the bushes by your house. I could not believe what happened. I just hid and hoped it would go away."

Even while swimming in the currents of the night's trouble, he thought about how he had just made Kryztof look good. He ran to help me, he had just told her.

"Do you know where he is?"

Tyszka leaned his head over his chest, and seemed to sob.

"I'm so sorry, Cecylia. I think he is dead. The machine gun fire was very intense. I don't know how anyone could have survived it."

"Oh, my God," she said in a thin whisper.

Cecylia sat by his side in the silence that was required to endure the recalibration of their lives if this were true.

Finally, she spoke. "Tyszka, we must find out what happened to our friend. Please, go now to his father's house to see if he knows. Then come back to me here."

"But, there might be German soldiers walking around. To find the other person, me."

"I don't think so. If they were, you know their ways, they would be pounding on doors to look inside for you."

"But, what if he is all right? If he's all right, I will be unnecessarily worrying his father. I can't do that."

"Tyszka, stop it, stop finding excuses. Go and do your duty."

There was no love in her eyes. Before they turned to disgust, he went.

The road to Mr. Penkalski's house was lined with the bogeymen that populate a mind filled with fear. Behind each shadow was the Gestapo, and every night critter's noise was the informer.

Tyszka looked through the window pane into the kitchen where he could see the old man sitting in a rocking chair next to a candle that lit up the room. He seemed to be talking to himself. The odd juxtaposition of a rocking chair next to a kitchen table caught the illustrator's eye.

It was late at night, a time in the little village when quiet was always respected. That, coupled with Tyszka's agitation, created an inner ambiance that was strange. He didn't know whether to pound his agitation into the door or to tap his respect onto the window pane.

He tapped the pane. For what seemed to be forever. The tiny hammer of his index finger began to hurt, while the noise seemed to grow louder with repetition. Just as he was about to go, Kryztof's father looked up and saw him. Tyszka beckoned to be let in.

"Mr. Penkalski, I don't know how to say this." He stopped to see a reaction that might warn him about how to handle the old man. He waited. Yet, only a nuance of his presence showed up.

"Your son, Kryztof, did not come to meet me and Cecylia tonight. He is always reliable, so this is strange. Do you know where he is?"

"Who are you?" he answered.

"I am Tyszka, Cecylia's friend. And a friend of your son. I live in the village. I am the illustrator."

"Well, yes. Thank you for coming. Do you know why my shops are closing up?" And then, in a whisper, he asked, "Why are they taking away all of our tractors?" as if the young man standing before him was a representative of Nazi Germany who might tell him about a collusion he didn't understand.

"Go to bed, Mr. Penkalski. I'm sure Kryztof is all right."

The look in the father's eye was one Tyszka had been noticing more and more lately in the village. Tonight it appeared to reach the final sweep of the charcoal pen in his mind's eye. He had never before drawn this look in the eyes. How could he draw what was not there?

10.

After Tyszka told Cecylia about the dentist's father, she asked him to go home so she could think about what had happened and how they could find out more. It was late, she told him, and they both needed rest. She asked him to be careful.

He tip-toed up to his room so as not to awaken his father. He sat down to read the note he had clutched for so long before putting it into his pocket while running to Cecylia's house.

Whoever you are, it began, we are grateful to you. We think of you as a friend who thinks of us. Each barrack takes a turn with the food you leave. We divide the potatoes and vegetables you leave by the number of people in the barrack. Shoulder to shoulder, we eat the food together at night and celebrate you for giving us the gift of togetherness, if only for a day.

Normally, Tyszka would not give himself over to sentiment. But there was this night, Kryztof, the bitter cold, the fatigue. Most of all, a sense that he was now living beyond the frontiers of his normally quiet life. It was a place of singular discomfort. Yet, the letter made him happy. For the first time ever, he felt pride in something other than his talent for depicting people's souls on paper. By helping the prisoners with food, he had taken up the pebble of his mother's indignation, and had thrown it into the pond.

After the guards dragged Kryztof in the mud through the open gate of the electrified fence, he was ordered to get up. A tough, snarly looking Gestapo officer, dressed in a smart black uniform, grabbed him by the jacket lapels, squeezing them together as if to collapse his chest into his heart.

A rough pat-down included grabbing his crotch hard enough to draw the desired scream. "Come with us," the crude man muttered as if inviting him to a party.

They brought Kryztof to Barracks No. 13. He was pushed through a front door that looked like it belonged to a red-bricked building in the elegant section of many of the numerous towns in Poland. The inside, though, was bare. Dimly lit corridors were lined with small cells. At the end of the passageway there was a room, three-feet across by six-feet high. A black water pipe ran across the top and another one diagonally down about two-thirds of the way up. There was an iron door with a large peep hole, and the walls were made of marble.

The metal door was opened, and Kryztof was met by the smell of fresh excrement seeping through the pants of a prisoner sitting on the floor. Two others who were standing next to him.

"You will spend the night here with them. Make your own arrangements."

The door was banged shut and he was alone with three strangers.

"I am Kryztof Penkalski from the village. Who are you?" he asked to no one in particular.

"I am Michal Jarkowski from Warsaw," answered the man standing closest to him.

The other standing man said simply, "I am from Radom," while the one sitting in his own feces was too embarrassed to talk.

"Why are you here?" the dentist asked.

In what seemed like a concert of solidified confusion, they responded, "Because we are Jews."

Naturally, the three who were standing decided to stay that way for the night. Two of the three, including Kryztof, found a clean place to stand on the cement floor. Each of the three leaned his back against the wall to support the weight of his body as best he could. They decided during the night to shift counter-clockwise about every hour. In this way, they would take turns standing in the waste, and be able periodically to rest their forearms and elbows against the diagonal water pipe. At least, they could relax the muscles of one leg every so often. It took Kryztof but one turn to figure out that in doing it this way only their left legs would be relieved. He asked that after each had taken one turn, they would switch the rotation clockwise. They agreed.

"You say that you have been arrested simply because you are Jews. I am a Jew, but I have not been arrested because I am a Jew."

"Then why?" asked the sitting man.

"I tried to help the prisoners in here by putting food under the fence, and I was caught."

"Ah, yes, but you are a Jew. Perhaps there was some hope for you if all you did was place food under the fence. But a Jew placing food under the fence for other Jews. Ah, I think there is no hope for you now."

"What do you mean?" he asked with a slight quiver in his voice. The dentist was an intelligent man, quick on the uptake of the streets, yet the parts of the equation for the German solution to their Jewish problem seemed to have eluded him during his frivolous pursuit to cultivate a successful practice. The infatuation with Cecylia sometimes made him unaware of the immediacy of the knot that was tightening around his neck. The transformational leap had occurred. What had been an intellectual awareness was now becoming a personal reality.

"Do you not know that Jews are being rounded up from all over Eastern Europe and put into places like this?" said the sitting man who was afraid to raise his voice to the level of his bubbling anger.

Krystof tried to respond, but the man grew louder.

"You say you live in Ocwiecim. Do you not see the trains coming to Auschwitz full and leaving empty? Do you not ask where all the people are going? You know they are Jews. You see the Star of David on their clothes. Do you not ask any questions about this? Do you read the underground newspapers? Talk with others who come into the village? Listen to their stories? The radio?"

The man's anger revved up and began to gush. Kryztof thought he smelled vomit, and shouted at the man to shut up.

Though nothing else was said among the four for the rest of the night, Kryztof knew he was in the kind of trouble that would take all of his cunning to escape.

11.

"So, you are Penkalski, the dentist."

"How do you know that?" he responded to the commandant.

"Do you think we are fools?" he whispered, as if trying to make Kryztof more nervous. "Surely you have noticed our SS in your village. They go there for many reasons, including strolling about for the shopping they seem to love. But they look, they notice. They are trained to notice, to size up their surroundings. They have reported to me about you, your soccer team, your practice. Do I say that right, your practice? That is what you call what you do, isn't it?"

The one-sided talk was too casual for the circumstances, and Kryztof began to feel more apprehensive.

"We know what you were up to last night, and we know who your companion was. Later we will ask you about him.

"For now, though, we want you to come with us outside. You may be of service to us. I must first put on my best uniform, the one I wear for formal occasions."

The commandant's adjutant, and two of the SS Death's Head guards accompanied the dentist to a special dead-end section of the camp, next to where he had spent the night, about a five-minute walk from Hoss's office.

Waiting for them was a wedding party, a bride in her white dress, the groom dressed in a black suit. Four members of the entourage, each dressed as nicely as they could for the ceremony that had been concluded yesterday in the church of St. Adalbert's in Krakow, stood nearby.

Commandant Hoss beckoned Kryztof to follow him to where the party was huddled together, grim-faced and frightened.

"Do you know why you are here?" he asked them. No one answered. To speak the answer would be too much to bear, especially during these days that had been designed for weeks with preparations to mark their marriage.

"Come here," he said. "Don't be frightened."

The newlyweds did as they were asked.

"You are a handsome couple. What are your names?"

The groom heard the question as his first call to leadership in the new partnership.

"We are Janina and Kazimer." He took a breath before boldly saying, "We are Janina and Kazimer Wandelt."

The commandant seemed personally affronted by the proud tone of the answer. He stared at Kazimer.

"Mr. and Mrs. Wandelt, Congratulations." Like a perfect gentleman, he extended his hand. Reflexively, both bride and groom reciprocated.

As they stepped away from the handshake, they both breathed a sigh of relief at the same time that Hoss unholstered his pistol. Lifting his right arm, he shot Janina directly through her forehead. She lurched upwards before falling on her back.

Kazimer, stunned, made a rush at the commandant, but the two guards overwhelmed him, smacking him on the head with their rifle butts. Others moved in to hold the members of the wedding party.

Immediately, Hoss instructed the guards to get the groom onto his feet. "Get at his side and hold him by his arms."

He whispered something into the groom's ear before sticking his pistol into the flesh of his stomach that muffled the two shots.

"They must learn that going to church is not allowed any more," he whispered to the gaping inmates who by now had gathered at the mouth of the corridor.

"Tie the others against the wall." While fixing the cuffs of his uniform, he said, "Shoot them!"

Gray cinderblocks lined the brick wall to protect it against stray bullets or shots that went cleanly through a victim. Sometimes, bored guards lined up prisoners here for target practice after lunch.

It was all over in a minute.

"Look at her, lying there," the commandant said to Kryztof who, by now, was frozen in shock.

"Sometimes when I shoot one of these unfortunates through the head, it makes a clean hole right through. But look at her, blood and brains scattered on that pretty white dress.

"You probably see lots of blood in your business, Herr Doctor. So this is nothing new to you," he said in a tone that beckoned for an answer that the dentist could not give.

"Come with me. I have what you might call a proposition for you."

12.

The commandant appeared nervous, a strange reaction for a man who had the power of life and death over others. After telling Kryztof to sit, he went to the large chair behind his desk and began to press the five fingers of one hand into the five of the other as if exercising them. He leaned over a bit, a slump in thought.

"You are a dentist, correct?" he finally said. Asking unnecessary questions with obvious answers was his way. Usually, he did not expect an answer, yet sometimes when one was not given he would get angry and demand it, as if not giving the answer was disrespectful to a man of his status.

He did not wait for a reply. "These people we just gave a special treatment to have been brought to the crematorium. Before people like them are burned to ashes, we like to look at their teeth to see if there are any gold fillings there. It is required."

He stopped for a moment, and began to press his fingers again before stealing a peek at the dentist. Kryztof noticed this reaction and his brain pounced on the words, knowing that for some reason they showed a weakness or a concern in the commandant about him. The man was cunning, though, so he did not know what this meant.

"I want you to go to the crematorium and see if they have any gold in their teeth. They were well-dressed, so they might. You know, the Jews love to have gold fillings. It's a way they have to make themselves feel superior.

"My adjutant, Lt. Kramer here, will go with you and provide any tools you might need to do the work. Remember, they are not your patients. They are dead and will feel nothing. Think of them like the dolls you practiced on in school when you were learning to pull teeth. They will feel nothing. Do you understand?"

The dentist nodded his head, as if reflexively assenting to something he did not understand but, like a child in school, was unwilling to admit it.

Lieutenant Kramer and two orderlies escorted Kryztof to the crematorium. The six bodies were lined up side by side on the cement floor. Janina Wandelt's blood-splattered white dress stood out. She seemed to be about the same age as Cecylia, and probably once as pretty. Now, though, the top part of her face was crushed and splintered, no longer recognizable.

"I need a snub-nosed dentist's pliers, and an extractor," he directed Kramer, as if the adjutant was his dental assistant. "I cannot do the work when they are on the floor. I have no leverage. I am not used to extracting in this position."

Kramer who was known, even among the inmates, for his lack of imagination, was used to getting his way by brute force and harsh directives, yelled, "Just do it. We just do it here."

Kryztof did not know where his resistance came from, except that he felt a sense that the commandant, for reasons unknown to him, wanted him around. He even imagined that Hoss indicated a certain deference to him.

He repeated, "I cannot do it this way. Get me a chair."

Kramer nodded to an orderly who ran outside and brought back a common wooden chair.

"Sit her up in it," Kryztof told the same man.

He did, but she fell over, her skull cracking like a broken egg on the floor.

"Take off your belt," he bellowed to Kramer, "and tie it around her chest so she stays put in the chair."

Although it was a simple matter to put her head back, it was not easy to open her mouth, now bloodied and growing stiff.

"Hold her mouth open for me," he directed the orderlies. One of them who had on a pair of thick canvas gardening gloves came by his side and twisted her mouth open by using the upper and lower bridges for leverage.

"Now let go and push hard on the jaw muscles to keep it open."

He looked to see if there was any gold in her mouth. Two remaining molars were filled with gold, a condition he knew that was more calculated to hide the precious metal than to preserve the teeth.

Though done more delicately many times in his office, extracting a tooth was never easy, as it was part of the bone. He wondered if the usual cracking sound would be the same to which he was accustomed.

The procedure was the same for each in the wedding party. Strap in the chair, look, pull.

He was told to put each of the gold-filled teeth into a metal bowl. After he was done, Kramer gave him a second, smaller bowl into which he was to place the gold that remained after he crushed the extracted teeth with a common pair of heavy pliers.

"Break them up as gently as you can, so none of the gold will be lost," he instructed the dentist, who did as he was told.

Were it not for his ability to shut out the pain of his professional betrayal and the loss of his dignity, Kryztof might have succumbed to an instinct to fall down right there and never get up again. Added to the weight of betrayal was the understanding that he was now materially complicit in something he could not comprehend but knew to be sinful.

Ever since he was a child, he knew how to dodge, even weave, around the truth. He had to know when to leave the house if his father was drunk and mean, or to stay when he was sober and silent. The skill was honed by the need to anticipate his father's condition this day, that night. It was a way to stay out of trouble.

Yet, it was the way to insincerity, the path to hide from himself and who he was. After a while, the only way of thinking he had was to calculate what actions he would take or words he might say that would keep him from being harmed. In this way, he never knew his own goodness nor his own capacity for evil.

Until today.

13.

It was two o'clock in the afternoon, an unusual time for Tyszka to be summoned to the commandant's office where he found Hoss touched by a nervous, quirky oddness.

Tyszka noticed that the arrangements and trappings of the office, though, hardly ever changed. Except for the pistol at its edge, the main desk was never burdened with the weight of paper work. This was set in neat piles on the smaller desk in the corner.

The always-present picture of Hitler was prominently displayed, as was an arrangement of yellow roses in a large vase of clear water on the same smaller desk. The only evident new thing was a framed memo from Himmler to Hoss that was placed near the spot where the commandant sat for his portrait.

"Good morning, Mr. Dunajski. Did you have a restful sleep last night?" he asked in a tone that suggested it was a real question.

As Tyszka had an almost preternatural ability to distinguish his own self-deception when it was itching to activate, he answered, "Yes, I did," knowing immediately the lie of his words.

"I am happy for you, then. Today, I am happy, too, for myself, that I am doing the work I came here for. I had an especially accomplished day yesterday, and I want you to draw me as I feel today," he said, trailing off into a whispered word, "happy."

"Yes, I want you to capture my happiness today. Let me first get into my dress uniform."

Tyszka had several minutes to prepare his paper and pens, his instruments of truth. It seemed like just seconds before Hoss was back, no longer in the mufti style he chose for doing office work. He was in his full SS lieutenant colonel's uniform, a sign that Tyszka knew to mean that there was something extra meaningful about today's illustration.

It was as if the Nazi was preparing a series of portraits of himself to officially inform the historical record of the next thousand years about his role in the fulfillment of the goals of the Third Reich.

This was a dreaded moment for Tyszka. Each subsequent time he drew Hoss he had to work harder at deception. The more brutal Hoss got, the more difficult it became for the illustrator to conceal the inexorable look of evil that permeated the commandant's face. Yet, he knew what the consequences would be if he depicted the truth.

He had seen consequences. One night, as he was being brought to Hoss's office for a session, the SS officer and guards stopped, possibly on orders, to watch an open fire pit being started.

The pit was long and deep, dug by prisoners, probably that afternoon. Large handfuls of straw were being dipped in gasoline and then lit near the edges of five pieces of wood, each of them being piled precisely between layers of bodies that had been killed in the gas chambers that afternoon. As soon as one row of five pieces of wood and five bodies was completed, another row was stacked next to it until the ditch was filled. Soon, the fat of the burning bodies began to stoke the fire with a hissing sound. A bit of flesh from one body that exploded from heated gas and air landed on Tyszka's arm. He covered his mouth with the crook of his other arm, yet the sourness of burning bodies slipped through his nose onto his tongue, now steeped in the taste of death. He began to feel nauseous.

"If the commandant is through with you in time, you will be able to see the exciting part of the burnings later," said one of the officers.

He did. What he remembered most was the chaos, shouting, wailing, and the whips. A truckload of women and children who had been processed and separated from the men at Birkenau were sent to Auschwitz that night, arriving about nine o'clock, just as Tyszka was being taken back to his house.

The fire he had seen being started when he arrived was by now roaring in full, intense flames. As soon as the truck pulled up to the gate, kapos pulled the children to one side. They were terribly frightened and tried to cling to their mothers. The guards began to beat them and the women with their whips, sometimes hitting one of the mothers in the breast or head with the blunt end of the handle.

The guards picked up the children and tossed them, by pairs when they were small enough, into the fire. It was over quickly. About twenty-five of them, he thought. Once their tiny bodies hit the hot flames and smoke, their screams were consumed like twigs in hot lava. Mothers, shocked and wailing, were herded into the barracks.

Yes, Tyszka knew consequences. He must be extra careful this afternoon with Hoss.

"Remember, now, I have brought you here today to draw my face in the black and white happiness I feel."

"Yes, Herr Commandant. I will be at my best today. I can see the joy in your face, and will capture it." As he set a clean sheet of paper on the makeshift easel, he dropped it. The quick, swiping motion he used to catch the paper knocked over the stand. He picked it up and re-set it quickly, trying to establish normalcy. "Please try to be as still as possible. In that way, I can catch every nuance of your high spirits."

As usual, one of the SS guards, trying hard to keep his eyes open and his head up, sat in a chair on the side of the room.

Tyszka was deliberate. He would first draw the colonel's gray hat, separated from a black visor by white cords, its top overly magnificent in a reach that was longer than the commandant's face. Tyszka often found this ludicrous, as if without the hat there would be no face. Or, it seemed to be an official prop that Hoss used to justified his actions. Tyszka did not know which. But it was important to get the height just right.

He was spared the difficulty when Hoss yelled to him, "Stop! I am going to do this today without my cap. I want the picture to show my entire face, the joy of it all."

With this, he placed his hat neatly on the desk, and resumed posing.

One would think that drawing Hoss's ears would be easy. It could not be that way for Tyszka who wondered if an ear is just an ear, or if it took a different form or shape after it had heard the screams of thousands of innocent people. He tried at first to draw them as the energy of the light they might exude passed to his own heart. But he could not, as there was so little light in them. If he accurately stroked the picture of the commandant's ears the way they appeared to him, they would show up on paper as shells of skin and cartilage without openings to hear.

Tyszka would have to find a new way to compromise his art without compromising himself. That would be difficult, but not too difficult, he hoped. To do this was like swimming against a strong tide. The harder he tried to work out what he thought were the concessions to his sixth sense about people, the more difficult it was for him to execute the adjustments in his art. It was as if his brain and its picture-taking mechanism was so tuned into the craft of his art that he could not simply will himself to self-deception. To get beyond today's hurdle, he decided to think of the lieutenant colonel's ears as having just heard the sounds of the tiny sparrows he and Cecylia sometimes fed with pieces of bread in his back yard. Or her voice itself which he so loved.

Tyszka almost got lost in this thought. Since adolescence, he was always attracted by the sound of a girl's voice. Without failure, he was also captivated by the girl behind the voice. After a while, he knew that the voice and the person were inextricably bound. Sometimes, when he was in line in a shop, he would hear a female voice behind him and know immediately if she was special to him. The lilt, the cadence? He did not know. He only knew that he had never heard a girl's voice that he liked without also discovering that he liked the girl. As time went by, he knew, too, that there was a direct relationship between how much he liked the voice and the intensity he felt for the girl.

As difficult as it was, he allowed himself to think of the ears in front of him as listening to the voice of beautiful Cecylia. The thought at least allowed him to depict ears that were more human than pink lumps sewn tight by evil deeds.

Hoss seemed to notice there that was something not wrong as much as slow about today's work.

"It is a busy time for me these days, Mr. Dunajski. Go faster! The trains are coming in, sometimes three a day with over six thousand Jews. I am busy handling my end of things. Do your work faster, more efficiently," he yelled.

Tyszka completed the ears without further trouble by telling himself that he was creating a new Hoss who could hear beautiful sounds.

Try as he may, though, he could not immediately transfer the same thinking to the man's eyes. Tyszka, the romantic artist, had always believed that a person's eyes revealed his soul. How could anyone who allowed children to be burned alive in fires be capable of seeing beauty? The illustrator concluded that if the commandant could see beauty for even a snippet of a second, it would be impossible for him to approve of the crimes he had directed.

Tyszka could see an emptiness in those eyes. How could he take out the lines of emptiness, and depict what is not there?

He decided first to draw Hoss's eyebrows which, he noticed, did not offend. True, they were accessories for his eyes, yet they did not seem useful. He never arched them to accommodate his brow when showing disapproval. The shrieking pitch of a tin voice did the work.

Ordinariness is not easy to depict. For the illustrator who was used to outlining the contours of innocence in babies, and whose own heart was beginning to discover its uniquely urgent capacities, showing parts of no exceptional quality, such as these eyebrows, called forth the finest nuances of his skills. Perhaps for the first time, Tyszka realized that he could easily shine a diamond, yet had trouble buffing the common rock.

He opted for simplicity. Like most black-haired men in their early forties, Hoss's eyebrows were still dark and a bit bushy at the peak just before they dove slightly to a thin end. Simple, yet Tyszka's carelessness made them appear undisciplined. The errant hairs had the appearance of barbed wire. Just then, the commandant, as was his way, asked him to stop so he could look at himself on the paper, always ready to critique the work.

"Stop! I want to ask you a question. First let me see what you have done."

Although he had not yet been hit or beaten at these sessions, Tyszka expected it now.

"You have done little. Too little," the commandant said, his voice beginning to rise. "You have drawn an empty egg with ears and eyebrows. Is that what you think of me? Can't you see the joy in my face today? Can't you see a man fulfilled?" He began to shout. "If you cannot see the joy, cannot do the work of showing it, maybe you are not what they say you are."

A pause seemed to settle down the commandant. Finally, all he said was, "The great illustrator!" before growing silent. "We will stop for today, as I see you are not up to it, and I have things to do. I have an hour tomorrow afternoon. Be ready when they come to your house.

"Before you go, I want to ask you something."

"Yes, Herr Commandant. What is it?"

Hoss rose and stood over Tyszka who was still sitting while gathering his materials.

"Before that, I want to tell you to keep your paper clean and in order. We will continue with this sheet tomorrow. Use the same one. I like the way my eyebrows look.

"Now the question. What do you think of Jews?"

Tyszka looked up, shock and fear on his face. The question was sudden and unexpected. It was charged, too, with possibilities for trouble.

"What do you mean?"

"I mean what I ask," he shouted. "What do you think of Jews?"

Tyszka knew that another delay in answering the question on top of a suspended drawing session might tax Hoss's patience.

"Some of my friends are Jews. They are friends, so that is how I think of them. As friends."

Talking with the commandant was like shuffling through a mine-field. One wrong word could explode the ground he walked on, yet he could not help but speak the truth.

"That is not enough, my friend," Hoss responded, as if trying to confuse the question with a casual declaration that he had just bestowed his own friendship on the man from Oswiecim.

"So your friends, some of your friends, are Jews. Take away that they are friends, and you are left with that they are Jews. Now what do you think of them as Jews?"

"Not more than I think of myself as a Pole who is Catholic."

Hoss seemed to be confused, and dismissed him.

14.

"I am told that you did a good job in extracting the gold from the bride and groom. I am told that you are good with your tools."

"Thank you, Herr Commandant," answered the dentist.

"You are not in a position to say no to what I am going to propose. Nevertheless, I am going to ask like a gentleman.

"Some of the gold that is being extracted from the teeth of Jews is being stolen by someone along the way, from teeth to the Reischsbank. From Auschwitz it goes to the Finance Department first. I have received orders to make sure that our side of the street is clean before the investigation is extended.

"Here is my proposal. That you take on the job of finding out if it is someone here who is the thief. I have chosen you because it is clear that you are new and untouched. Besides, you seem competent and composed. I noticed yesterday when I shot the couple that you did not flinch or try to run."

Less than two days ago, Kryztof was an ordinary dentist in a little town. Suddenly, he was being made an offer to collude with a killer, to be a detective assigned to finding a thief who robs gold from gold that is stolen.

He knew that he didn't have a choice, yet he wanted to place a good front on his answer.

"What do you expect of me?"

Before Hoss had a chance to answer the question, Kryztof asked another.

"What charges do you have against me? All I did was to bring a few vegetables to the prisoners."

"For a smart man, you sometimes act like you are stupid. You know I could have you shot for what you did. Even better, I could put you in one of the gas chambers at Birkenau before roasting you in one of our ovens. Do you know that it takes only sixty seconds to burn your body to ashes?"

The exchange was surreal in its softness.

"What do you want me to do?" the dentist asked.

"I have two jobs for you. The first is to find out if anyone here is stealing gold from the Third Reich. To do this, you will have to be at work, night and day. You will not get much sleep, but you will be in a special barrack with other Jews who do certain work for us, specialty work. You will be well fed, given alcohol to drink and, if you are inclined, you can sometimes use the camp brothel for your needs.

"I want you to get around, in and among the workers who prepare the bodies for cremation. Talk with them, find out what you can. Report only to me. No one else is to know about this.

"One more thing. One other job. I want you to experiment with the dead bodies to see if it is better to take out the teeth from their mouths before or after they are cremated.

"Find out which way is more efficient, both for time we spend on getting the gold, and for the amount of gold we get. We are all about efficiency here. I want to find out if we have a thief, and I want to have the best means of moving along the process of killing and disposal while keeping what is most valuable from the dead Jews.

"You will report to me every three days. Unless, of course, you make a discovery about the thief. Then, you will come to me immediately. Do you understand my proposal?"

"Yes."

"Do you accept?" he asked with a quick shift of his head downwards, as if bowing to the obvious.

"I do."

"Good. Now sit down. I have a few questions for you about your 'vegetable trips' to the fence."

Hoss was about to test out on the dentist a few of his own private thoughts about Jews.

He had never been demonstrable about his feelings toward Jews, although he had once told a colleague that he "loathed" them. Like so many others, he knew that career advancement was certain if his actions echoed Hitler's words about Jews.

Many times at parties he would tell friends about the first time he saw Hitler speak, at a park in Munich in 1934. The commandant was always pleased to say that, although he had been indifferent toward Jews before that day, he became fired up with hatred for them after listening to his Fuhrer. He was certain that a man of Hitler's growing stature and intellect must be correct when he concluded that

Jews were behind the rise and spread of Communism that would take over the German state if the Jews were not eliminated, and that Jews were behind the depression, hoarding the millions they made off the Volk. It was said with such conviction, Hoss thought that it must be true. The more he heard that the Jews were vermin to be eliminated, the more he believed that the words were an unyielding expression of the truth.

Among his colleagues, having heard Hitler speak in person became, in time, the touchstone for the authenticity of one's anti-Semitism. They talked about the experience as if the words he spoke had floated across the air, seeping into their brains before settling into the deepest recesses of their souls.

Although he never experienced Jews as the smelly vermin depicted by Hitler, he also became infected with hatred. On the day that his wife discovered the nature of his work, she asked him why. He answered "Because Heinrich, head of the Gestapo, asked me. It was so natural."

Besides, he thought, she had never heard Hitler speak. If she only had, she would know why.

15.

"Dr. Penkalski, you are a Jew. A dentist. A Jewish dentist, you might say."

The dentist knew that much was a stake here today, perhaps even his life. That if he didn't answer each question precisely according to the wishes of this man, he could be summarily executed or, perhaps worse, have the few privileges he was given so far taken away.

"What do you think of Jews?"

"I am sorry, Herr Commandant," he answered, unaware that he was repeating Tyszka's reply to the same question. "I don't know what you mean."

"You intellectual people are all the same. You play with words, don't you?"

Kryztof guessed right to answer the question, and to give a satisfactory answer: "Yes, we do."

Without waiting, he continued, "I am sorry." Again, perfect. An obeisance paid.

"So, now that we have established the nature of your game, tell me, what do you think of Jews?"

"You know, of course, Herr Commandant, that I am a Jew myself. I have been brought up with other Jews. I know their beliefs, though I do not go to the synagogue."

"What do you think of Jews?" Hoss repeated, as if he was trying to find the answer to a nagging question.

"They are people who live and work in Poland, in Oswiecim."

"You speak as if they are just people, ordinary people who live only in Poland. I did not ask where they lived or where they worked."

Penkalski would be careful, very careful.

"I know they live in other places. I just thought you meant what do I think of them around here."

"Okay, let's play the game. We'll leave it at that, around here. So, then, you!" shouting the word *you*. "Hear me ask the question again."

After a brief silence, the dentist replied, "Yes, Herr Commandant. I will answer the question. They are a special people, in the same way as Germans are special people. By that I mean they have a distinct expression of their identity."

"Yes, go on. But why do you compare them to Germans? Germany is a nation, Jews are a race of people."

"Herr Commandant, if I may say, I have read that the Fuhrer thinks that Germans come from a pure race of people who are destined to lead the world."

The dentist realized he was stepping into uncomfortable territory.

"But, getting back to the Jews," he said, "they have a long history. They are very cultured and good at what they do," adding, "in the same way that Germans are good at what they do."

"What do you mean, good at what they do?"

"I mean they know how to get things done, the way you know how to get things done here in the camp."

"You are a good dentist. You are also a good sparring partner with words. There is no one else here as good as you are. You flatter me, yet I like it when you do.

"But, go on. You say they have a long history, are cultured, and good at what they do. Go on, tell me."

Kryztof was good at this. For him, a conversation of this sort was a problem to be diagnosed, a difficult tooth to be pulled from a nest of overlapping teeth that wanted to keep the inflammation buried where it could continue to rot into other rows of teeth.

"Herr Commandant, the Jewish people go back thousands of years. I am not an intellectual, as you say I am, so I do not know for how long precisely. It is said thousands of years."

"So what, you say thousands of years. The German peoples have been here for thousands of years also. We are Teutonic."

"I am sorry, but I do not know what that means," Penkalski replied in a soft voice.

Hoss began to snicker, as if he were a little boy finding himself caught uttering words he didn't understand. The giggle suddenly burst into full-blown laughter. Kryztof did not know how to react, to laugh along or stay sober-faced. Instead, he showed a glimmer of a smile, so faint that it was open to interpretation.

Again, he guessed right. Just at the height of his laughter, when his usual vacant eyes seemed like they might break into tears, the commandant bellowed, "I don't know either!"

With some hesitation, the dentist's smile grew wider.

"Now that we are done with that, let's see, where were we? You were saying how cultured the Jews are. Tell me, what does that mean, cultured?"

The conversation was beginning to normalize itself, or so the dentist thought. Just as he began to speak of the contributions German Jews were making to the nation, Hoss cut him off so abruptly that the tone was immediately changed, and charged with danger.

"You say the Jews are good at what they do. What they do is bring the German nation to ideas that are indecent. Their expression of dance is vulgar. The art is lewd. The theater is full of ideas. Their rituals with candles and scrolls are ridiculous. And they are always referring to this God of theirs, their, how do you say, adoney?"

"It's Adonai," he replied, seeing the word in his mind, but afraid to contradict.

"Whatever it is." After a pause, he asked, "Do you ever see this God? Who is this God? Where is he?"

"The Jews think Adonai is everywhere."

"I can tell you one thing for certain, my dentist friend. Your adonai is not here in Auschwitz." He picked up the phone on his desk. The conversation was over for now.

"Today, you become official."

Unlike the mass tattooing of prisoners who were saved from the imediacy of the gas chamber, Kryztof was given special consideration on this day. One of the camp tattooers

was escorted into the office. The SS guard who accompanied him ordered Kryztof to pull up his sleeve. The needle,
much used and full of black ink, was painful in an odd sort
of way, unlike any sensation he had ever had. He felt as if
he was on the verge of pain, yet without the pain, as if the
needle head itself was the edge of pain.

"Let me see," said Hoss, as soon as the job was over. "Ah,
yes, you are now number 011653."

"Herr Commandant, I don't know what this means."

"It means you are a Jew inside Auschwitz."

16.

It was as if Kryztof had disappeared. Tyszka and Cecylia knew what happened at the fence and where he must be, although they knew nothing else.

"I feel so bad. He was just trying to help. It should have been me."

"It wasn't you, Tyszka. And it wasn't your fault. We must think if there is a way that we can get him out." A light came into her eyes. "There is a way, I think. You have told me that you have been illustrating a series of portraits of the camp head. You could meet with him and ask him about Kryztof. Maybe if he values your work, he will let him go."

"But how would I ask the commandant without revealing that I know him or what happened at the fence? If I do that, then maybe I am done too. I think I am valuable to Hoss only as long as he needs me to do his picture."

"That is precisely the point. You are valuable to him and he will listen to you. You must keep him interested."

She got up from the chair near the window in Tyszka's room, and walked toward him. She seemed determined. Whenever she got like that, Tyszka's heart swelled. He admired determination in women. He didn't know why he liked it, but when he saw it in a woman to whom he was also attracted, it took on an idealized worth that was sometimes disproportionate to its value. He knew this about himself.

"My dear Tyszka, you must do this. If not for Kryztof, then for me." She bent down toward him, and kissed him lightly on the forehead.

He did not know how, in times like this, to separate her charm from her resolve. Whenever she wanted something from him that he did not appear to want to give to her, a favor, a small task, she tried to get his cooperation by being flirtatious. Always, she became playful, and at the same time, with a certain intuitive genius, she listened to him talk. He loved the ways she had of listening to him, making him feel that someone was for the first time hearing him, for the first time understanding how he saw himself. For a woman to listen to a man's story, ah, there was genius.

With his own cunning, he would seize these opportunities to reveal himself to her. So while she was hearing the story of his inner life, he had a chance to insinuate to her how he loved her. It was only in these moments when she tried to charm him that Tyszka was allowed to get honest about the extent of his thoughts for her and the depth of his feelings.

It was a wonderful game they played. She needy and playful, he expressive, though in a coded sort of way. How perfect for him, for whom the language of love was terrifying with the threat of rejection, to tell her of his longing to be with her. If she was as complete as Tyszka thought her to be, she might not have been able to bear her own presence.

When she leaned over to kiss him today, he wondered if there could be anyone else in Oswiecim, or Poland, or even the world, who was as beautiful as she. The brunette of her hair seemed different from all others. No one could wrap it in a bun with a certain flair, he thought, with just enough strands hanging free to balance the tight weave of the knot that held it all together.

Even with training in the craft of artistic nuance, he could never decide what was the color of her skin. Perhaps it was an off-shade of cream, perhaps a light-yellowish tan. In either case, he found her skin to be so clear, as to have a kind of luminescence coming from underneath it. It was as if there were a new kind of light, with a new way of showing itself, that lined the inner skin of her face. The beauty of this light shone through just enough in the same way that nature itself allows just the right amount of sun to shine through to reveal the wonder of Earth.

Every now and then, for the past several years as he noticed his attention being drawn toward her in a narrowing circle of people and things that mattered, he would allow himself to imagine, in a fantasy complete with ritual, the rest of her body and how she might look naked.

He always began with her face, the most vivid part for him. All he had to do was picture in his mind a line of sunlight crossing the slight swell of her left cheek. Without effort, the image would quickly enter the alchemy of his imagination where he could see the fullness of breasts made sweaty by the same sun. It was easy for him to move down the slim bottleneck of her hips to down between her legs.

Whenever he got to that place, he would stop. In the fantasy, he could never get her underpants off, as they would become entangled in her feet. He could not continue, bothered not by what he was about to do, but by her not knowing in their real lives what he was thinking and imagining. It made him feel deceitful.

"Cecylia, it is always so good to be with you. To talk with you. I am hesitant to tell you today that I am frightened of what is happening around here. If I tell you my dread, you will think less of me."

He began to calculate, a way of being that he hated about himself because he thought it interfered with his art which must express itself purely. An illustration without purity was for him a lie. To whatever degree he began to calculate in his daily life and relationships, to that same degree his work suffered.

Yet, he began to calculate with Cecylia. He could not help it, as the training of an entire lifetime, short as it was thus far, hindered his self-expression except as it showed up in his art.

He must figure out how far to reveal himself to Cecylia so she might never see his human side, or low side which he had been taught by the nuns and priests to be dishonorable and bad. Self-revelation in conversation must be allowed to expose only his good side, for only that side was loveable. Winning over someone wonderful such as Cecylia, he knew, was almost impossible for him to do. He must, then, be careful of everything he revealed about himself, to show only the side that might attract someone as good as she.

In recent months, as his feelings deepened for her, he figured out a way to get over the loss of good face whenever he inadvertently stumbled over the line to reveal a less favorable side of himself. He would simply express indifference when he became weary under the weight of trying so hard to impress her.

At these times he resorted to listening as much as he could, which became another way to impress her. She, perhaps more than most people, liked to be heard. Her center was large and filled with a certain self-preoccupation that matched her need to express it. This way of being often informed the content and range of her conversation. So, there was much for Tyszka to be quiet about, to just listen. It was a way of communicating with her that he embraced as it had its rewards. Another dollop, he hoped, in the chemistry of love.

"Tyszka, We need to talk."

Whenever he heard those words from her, his heart skipped so hard that he could feel it in his chest. He knew that something important was on her mind, sometimes about their relationship. Tyszka noticed over the years that every now and then she needed to reinforce with him that she considered him to be a great friend. She would use words like "love" and "respect," which always warmed him, yet the way she combined them would leave him cold.

"You are my dear friend, Tyszka, whom I love and respect," she would say in her educated and formal way, and he'd think if she only would say, "You are my friend, Tyszka.

I love you." To be a "dear" friend was, nevertheless, just a friend, a close one at that, but not what he wanted to be.

And, to be respected . . . well, she respected her parents, her teachers, the rabbi. Too many people for it to mean anything special about him.

He noticed, too, that she took pains to formally reestablish that he was her dear friend when her mother's weariness was upon her, or when the impact of the Nazi invasion became an immediate concern, such as the edict to wear the Star of David on her sleeve. Or the need to get permission to visit her friends from the university in Posnan.

What he did not understand, in the constant and self-inflicted negative comparisons with her, was that he had become a rock for her, a place where she could stand, at least for a brief spell, and be secure in her footing. He did not understand the great gift he was to her. Though she knew, she had yet to express it to him.

17.

Although it was clear to the dentist that the commandant respected him, perhaps even liked him, he did not trust the nature of the relationship. How could he? Whatever Hoss needed, it seemed to Penkalski, he had at his fingertips. A family, house, food, power, money, influence. He could not fathom why he was being befriended. Nor could he do anything about it. When he was called, he went quickly.

In the dozen or so times he called the dentist to his office to speak, the commandant became increasingly at ease in talking openly about the management of the camp. He did not seem to care about the implications of what he was revealing. He was, too, indifferent that he was talking to a Jew.

"Do you know, Dr. Penkalski, that we are quite efficient here in what we do? We are proud of our part in the solution to the problem that has met us. Every day now, we kill and burn more and more Jews. Our problems with others are being solved too."

How does one respond?

"We now kill thousands in the gas chambers each day. We burn them in the trenches and ovens, 12,000 a day. Of course, that is when we are coordinating each part of our operation. Sometimes, carloads of the wretches come in so fast that we quickly separate those who are useful for work and kill those who are not, such as children and the weak.

"As you can see, the barracks and stables are over-crowded, so we must keep on turning them over."

Hoss began to crack his knuckles. So fast that the dentist thought they would explode.

"We have trained some Jews and Poles to work the ovens, so that now, I am proud to say, it takes only a little over a minute to incinerate each body. Our efficiency, though, has caused two problems," he said, as if echoing his recent monthly report to the high command in Berlin. "There is, of course, the accumulation of ashes from the bones. We use much of this to fertilize the farm which you might have already noticed is on the far north end of the camp. The rest we throw into the fires that burn in the trenches. Some into the river.

"Our other problem is the efficient collection and disposal of their goods, their possessions. As well as the part you know, the gold in the teeth.

"We do a good job of this. The clothing we use for some of the prisoners in the labor force. You know where the gold goes."

In a strange expression of intimidating humor, he added, "At least I hope you do." Adding "We sort the rest, bags, watches, shoes, women's compacts. Have you noticed that they like to use valuable compacts for their faces? No good to them now. If only they had their funerals. We make use of everything. Even the hair on Jewesses."

Pointing the tip of his knuckle-fatigued right index finger at the equally fatigued doctor, he said, "You see, I know the word for a female Jew. I am impressive, wouldn't you say?"

A nod.

"Do you know what we do with this hair?"

"No, commandant."

"It is woven into special fittings for gaskets."

He then looked at Penkalski as if to await a word of approval for the vision of his work.

"What do you think of our efforts?" he asked, as if he was toying with the dentist, who hoped it was one of those questions that need not be answered.

Penkalski breathed deeply and simply said, "I don't know."

Hoss expressed the tiniest smile of annoyance before responding.

"So, you have nothing to say. Actually, I do not expect you to answer. I am sensitive to your feelings about the matter." He walked across the room to get his riding crop.

Before exiting the room for his daily inspection, he turned and said, "What we are doing here is correct and necessary."

18.

It would not seem possible to beat someone to death with a riding crop. It is, after all, light enough by design for a man to carry in one hand, and flexible enough to exclude the bluntness necessary to punch through skin.

In his quiet hatred today, Hoss managed to achieve the impossible in the realm of sadism. His usual equestrian inspection of the camp began differently. The difference was obvious to prisoners who knew horses. Except for the most stubborn, they reflected the will of their rider. And since Hoss chose only the most docile horses, it was clear that the mood of the commandant this day smelled of anger.

His horse abandoned the rhythmic gait to which prisoners were accustomed. Once, Hoss had the same horse follow a mad dog that was chewing a two-year-old child to death in front of everyone for clinging to her mother at separation time. When the dog finished with the pulp of the child, its master pulled it away and calmed it down before trotting the dog off to the kennel. Hoss looked at the body of the dead child for a minute before pulling on the reins to go off in the opposite direction.

There was little rhythm in the horse today. Its gait was that of an animal infected with zig-zag. Its trot was a stagger, the almost mindless meandering of a drunk. Then suddenly a gallop before a slow walk. Yet, the horse and the rider were one, a seamless movement of man and beast.

The need to merge with his animal, to feel his anger in a roiling synchronization, was suddenly interrupted by a middle-aged prisoner, a woman who had about her the delicacy of one who was used to a life padded by privilege.

She jumped in front of the horse, pleading with the commandant about an ache in her tooth.

"Herr Commandant, I have had a pain in my tooth for many days now. It pains like a knife, and no one will do anything for me. I beg of you to help me."

Hoss tried to steer his already erratic colt from bumping into her as she continued to move in front of him to get attention.

"Get out of my way, you fool," he began to yell at her. She would not stop darting in and out of his way.

After several louder commands, he yelled to a kapo to get her out of his way. The man tried, but the woman grew more hysterical, as though the camp head was the only one who might help her.

"Please, Herr Commandant, please help me. Get me a dentist. The pain is too much. I need your help."

He began to hit her in the face with his riding whip, hoping it would drive her away. What he did not know about himself was that his will to hate was about to be unhinged. Her plea for help was for him a nagging whimper from a woman whose helplessness and weakness he could not stand.

As she covered up her face from the quick welts of the whip, she continued to implore him for help, and his anger slipped beyond the boundaries of self-control.

He got off his horse, which then began to scamper in circles, but there was no one to rein it in.

Hoss began to hit the woman some more until they began to synchronize. The more she pleaded, the more he hit her. Now with wild, powerful swings that struck her first in the face, then in her stomach, he began to scream at her, "Shut up, shut up." With each lash of the crop, he yelled so that a rhythmic cadence was set up. Each word of the relentless command was met with another stroke to her face and body.

"Shut" met by a hit, then "Up" by another. He was beating her as if in tune with some inner song of evil that gave him strength.

Blood began to squirt from her nose and eyes. Then from her mouth. Yet, he continued to whip her until he bent to one knee, the anger for now consumed in the violence of his whipping.

He looked up at the small crowd of prisoners and guards that gathered to witness the execution.

"Get her out of here," he said to no one in particular.

19.

For several weeks now, Kryztof had little to report to Hoss about the missing gold. He was but one of several dozen dentists assigned to the job of extracting gold from the teeth of dead prisoners. Yet, the only one that he was aware of with the assigned task of trying to find out if anyone was stealing gold.

He did report to the commandant that he thought it was better to get gold fillings from the dead before they were incinerated. After the fire, he reported, the jaw bone was almost burned to ashes that would mix into the gold.

He thought the report self-evident, yet it did not please Hoss because carrying out its recommendation required more administrative work for him. He would have to demand from Eichmann a precise anticipation of the numbers of Jews who would be transported to Auschwitz each day. In this way, the commandant, who knew how many bodies the crematorium might handle on any given day, could calculate the number left over who must be burned in the pits that same day. Work schedules must be arranged.

"I have not seen anything unusual about the missing gold except for the actions of one of the Sonderkommandos, an orderly whose name is, I think, Maier. Finkelstein, I think. But, again, I am not sure. If I try to get his name, he might get suspicious of me and then hide his actions.

"I could try to get his number for you but, again, he might grow suspicious."

"Tell me what he does that is different."

"It is usual for prisoner orderlies to keep their actions consistent, so that no one will think there is anything out of the ordinary about them. The group that is under my supervision must wear gloves, the lightest possible, so that they do not contract any diseases from the dead people's mouths. You know, the mouth is filthy.

"I do this now for the sake of the system and how it operates. If one of the *Sonderkommandos* gets diseased and dies, I must seek out a new one. That and the training necessary wastes time for the system. So, I try to keep them well."

It did not take much time for Kryztof to make himself at home in the system. When he first went into the crematorium several weeks ago to work a regular shift, the work was revolting to his sensibilities. For a while, he felt his way around jaws of the dead rather than look into their mouths as he was trained to do.

As the days went by, he thought at first that the only way he could get through his assignments was to work as fast and efficiently as possible. In this way, he could transfer the revulsion he felt to pulling gold from dead people's mouths to a sense of personal effectiveness. It was a way to keep his mind off the horror of what he was doing.

He knew, too, that implementing a way for the *Sonderkommandos* to keep from being infected with disease was collaborating doubly with the wrongdoing of stealing gold from the murdered. In time, though, he told himself that he was preventing the spread of disease, and that this was a good thing.

Smirking, Hoss replied, "I am impressed. But, tell me now, what does this Maier man do that arouses your suspicion?"

"Every now and then, maybe every two days, I am not sure, I do not keep records. He takes off the gloves and turns his back into the table where we now do our work. When he does that, I notice that he puts his hand down into his striped pants and onto his backside. I noticed this several times. I have said that. Then I asked him what he was doing.

"He wanted to know what I meant. When I told him about putting his hand down his pants, he explained to me that he had a ticklish anus. That the itch was something he had since he could remember. That there was no cause for alarm, he was not sick. But, I am not sure."

Trying to stay calm in the presence of the calculating dentist was difficult for Hoss.

"Why don't you get sure?" he asked in a tone that was half a question, half an order.

"I thought about that, but when I suggested to him to let me see his problem, he said I would not like the smell, that he did not often shower because he was afraid his clothes might be stolen."

"So, let me see here. What you've got so far is Maier Finkelstein who doesn't shower much, scratching an itchy asshole."

"I am sorry, sir, that I do not have more to tell you. But you did order me to report even the slightest questions I might have about anyone."

"Yes, so I did."

With the decisiveness of a man who cannot tolerate ambiguity, Hoss told him to get a flashlight, take two guards with him and, on his authority, find the man, pull down his pants and investigate the possibilities.

"When should I do that, sir?"

"Now, right now, you idiot."

As Kryztof began to flee the office, Hoss called him back.

"I am sorry, Herr Doctor. You are not an idiot. But, go now, do what I have told you."

"What shall I do if there is gold in that place?"

"Show it to me. Be certain it is clean."

20.

Maier Finkelstein was resting in his bunk when they found him.

"Get up," the SS guard yelled at him.

He did and was immediately spun around, then ordered to put both hands on the wood of the upper bed. Then they ripped his pants down around his ankles.

"Bend over!"

"I am sorry, I do not mean you harm," Kryztof heard himself saying.

By this time, a small crowd of fellow kapos was beginning to watch, assembling around the bunk, expecting to find a new horror.

"I knew this dentist was a homosexual," said one.

"No, he cannot be. They are separated and in the Birkenau camp."

"You are fools. They are everywhere in the camp. Do you not see, do you not hear in the night?"

One of the guards gave Kryztof a rubber glove. He knew what to do.

"You are lucky, my friend. There is no gold. Do both of us a favor, and stop scratching yourself."

Kryztof pulled off the glove and threw it on the floor. He immediately went to report his findings.

"Herr Commandant, we have made the inspection. There is no gold there."

"I hope you are certain. It is not in your best interests to be uncertain. Keep watching for two more weeks, and then I will send my report to Berlin. Be certain. I do not want my reputation to be undermined."

"Yes, I understand."

Kryztof backed up as if to leave, but did not as he had learned that no one leaves the camp commander's presence without first being dismissed.

"Come here. I want to show you something."

As the dentist walked closer, Hoss began to brush his uniform collar and shoulder area. Several gray flecks fell to the ground.

"Look at my new mirror," he said while sweeping his right arm and hand in a rising arc toward where a large rectangular mirror, almost as tall as a man, was hanging on the wall.

He seemed bitten with a small pride in showing it off to Kryztof, as if his opinion bore some importance.

"Come, come. Stand in front of it and see yourself. You can see almost all of yourself in it."

He did what he was told, although he never was as interested in looking at himself as the commandant was.

"What do you think?" Hoss asked.

"It is a very nice mirror, Herr Commandant. I hope you have many happy hour—I mean I hope you have many times. What I mean to say is I hope you enjoy the mirror, that it serves your purpose."

"Thank you, Dr. Penkalski. Would you like to know what that purpose is?" After a pause, he said, "I will tell you.

"I have had trouble recently seeing myself. I don't mean only seeing myself in a mirror. I am not having difficulty in seeing, you know. What I mean is seeing myself for who I am."

He began to pace a little in a circle, as if he were on a merry-go-round of thinking that might remain uncluttered as long as it moved.

"When I dress in my full colonel's uniform, with my decorations, my belt and holster, my boots a shiny black, my cap, I see myself as a representative of the Reich, the Fuhrer. Every part of me burns with what I am accomplishing here, and how I do it."

He stopped circling and went over to the mirror. He spread his legs slightly and put his hands behind his back.

"This will not do," he said, and quickly withdrew into a side room. When he came out, he was in full dress uniform.

"I must put on my uniform to tell you what I mean."

The dentist did not understand why Hoss confided in him. By now, though, he had learned to accept it.

"Look at me, Herr Doctor. Do I not look splendid? I especially like the way the smallest color in my medals contrasts to the tight black of my uniform, the way the shine of my belt, holster, and boots catch the light. So I look together, my parts very secure with each other."

Pulling the sides of his jacket down with his hands, he tucked both middle fingers under the belt, sliding them along front to back to front again in order to create a new snugness around his waist.

He turned to Kryztof, waiting for a response.

"You do strike a pose, Herr Commandant. A wonderful pose, efficient and powerful."

"Yet, when I take off my uniform, I see myself, I see myself . . . well, not the same way. Let me show you."

He again went to the side room, and when he came out he was dressed in a pair of brown cotton pants, a white shirt with long sleeves, and common black shoes.

"Now, when I look in the mirror, I see someone different. I look into my face and I'm not sure who I see. I look and look again, and I think I see myself as my wife and children see me."

On an intuition, Kryztof responded, knowing why the commandant was confiding in him. He was certain now that he was a person positioned in Hoss's alignment of people somewhere between the bureaucrats who persuaded his professional life and the few who loved him. He was placed somewhere, in effect, between Hitler and the commandant's family.

"How do they see you, Herr Commandant?"

"I am not certain. My children, of course, see me as their father. Even though they live close by, they have no idea what goes on here. So, we have a normal relationship. They are only four and two years old. They play with me when I go home. I play with them. Occasionally, when I take a

108

holiday, I go with them for a picnic in the Tatra Mountains. My children are wonderful.

"It is my wife, though," he said as he began to pace around the room, pressing all the fingers of each hand against the corresponding ones of the other, tweaking them against each other. Each time he pressed them together, he would allow them to remain together, as if the ten fingers had just become five.

Each time, too, when they would release and become ten, he would quickly press them together again. When he did this, he looked to the dentist as if he were praying.

"She has told me that she does not want to stay here anymore with the children, that she does not like it here. And what we do."

He now looked to assess if there was any interest in what he was saying.

The cunning Penkalski, with a slight upward tilt of his head, indicated his undivided attention.

"Some days this is difficult for me. I would like to please her, and I can see why she does not like what we do here. She does not fully understand. If she did, she would not ask questions.

"I can understand her point of view. Which really is not a point of view as we know that term. A point of view, to be valid, must be based on something real, even important. She thinks that what we do is, well she has said to me that it is bad.

"I can see from a certain, shall we say point of view, that what we do here is different. It is a camp that provides workers to German industry. What I do is keep our camp free from disease and weakness. My job is to see that whenever there is sickness to get rid of the germs, to keep the camp as disease free for the workers as I can.

"I have even instructed Dr. Mengele to have him and his doctors select only those strong enough and old enough to be our workers, to provide the labor we need to crush those who oppose us.

"I do not reject the fact that, on a very good day, we get rid of twenty-thousand of the opposition here in Auschwitz. It is the same as if we were bombing the enemy in their homes. The difference is that here it is more swift and less bloody.

"I do not think that my wife will ever understand that. She remains, though, a good wife and mother. All she asks of me is to send them back to Berlin where they can live with her mother.

"I think I will do that soon. I do not want to look at her anymore. Whenever I see her in the evening, I cannot help wanting to come back to this mirror and look again. I think she thinks, without saying so, that what I do is not good.

"So, I have begun lately to look into the mirror to find the 'bad man.' I tell you, though, I cannot find him. Do you know why?" he asked Penkalski.

"Well, sir, perhaps it is because he is not there."

"You are right. For a moment there, at the beginning, when I was helping to set up the first camps, I had a thought that bad things might happen. Then I began to realize, especially when I heard the Fuhrer speak, that it was a good thing for Germany if those things happened."

He turned to the dentist, and suddenly became the camp commandant again. Any self-doubt he seemed to have disappeared as quickly.

"Leave here now. If you tell anyone what I have just told you, I will shoot you on the spot. Do you understand?"

"Yes, Herr Commandant, I do."

"And by the way, we will speak soon about your friend at the fence."

As he was leaving, he stole a peek at Hoss who was again looking at himself in the mirror.

21.

Mid December weather in Oswiecim was much more severe than in November. Whenever Cecilia left her house, she felt as if the temperature and the water in the air had somehow compressed into each other so that it was not possible to distinguish the cold from the humidity. They had become one.

The gloom hanging over the small town was contagious. Dim spirits matched the grayness that saturated the days. If on a bright day one wore dark glasses to keep out rays that might hurt the eyes, the inhabitants of this town prayed for new and different glasses, ones that would expand the tiny shafts of mid-day sun into full rays of light that might lift the melancholy they felt in their souls.

It is an almost inexorable law of living that in the middle of secrecy and lies, some truth will be known. Often, time must go by before the manifestation. Occasionally, time speeds up so that truth becomes inextricably bound to the lie.

Such was the case in Oswiecim. The more the Germans pretended that the war was going well for them, the more certain the townspeople were that it was not going well.

The signs of this were apparent to Tyszka for whom the nature of things was always evident, as it could not be any other way for him.

He could feel the tension of contrary pulls permeating the social and economic intercourse of the town. Even though it was forbidden to have short-wave radios, hiding them in the undetectable nooks and crannies about the small, old houses was easy. Everyone knew about the progressively fast Soviet advances from the east, and that it was just a matter of time before they would be in Oswiecim.

There was not, though, a good feeling about the new army that would be coming through. In the same way that there was a general awareness that something bad was going on in Auschwitz, there was an apprehension that the intentions of the Red armies for Poland were not magnanimous. The mood was darkened by the eagerness of those who knew details about the camp to tell others, as well as those who knew, mostly by permitted travel to the cities, the larger political picture.

It was as if the tension had a life and a body with slimy tentacles that could penetrate the universe of being as it was made known in the town.

Things were out of alignment. The unusual was becoming the usual. How could it be that rooftops were whitened by human ashes? That the cindered remains of the burned bodies of children could be swept from sidewalks into little piles.

Shopping became tentative. The little hardware store was a bit overstocked as people were making up their minds whether to buy the nuts and bolts necessary to maintain their houses, or to save their money for a breakout from the "Mongols of the East."

Even parked cars were covered by a thin layer of human ashes. In the past week, someone wrote "Wir scheissen auf Deutche,"—*We shit on Germans*—in this dust on the hood of a car. It was quickly erased by an elderly man who knew there would be drastic consequences if it was discovered by a Nazi.

By this time, rubber was so scarce that anyone outside the camp who owned a car would remove the windshield wipers at the end of the day against their being stolen in the night.

The rule of gloom must be contested. Men would see to that in the two town taverns where they tried to revive their spirits. Sometimes, a few Waffen SS officers would come to drink, although they had ample liquor supplies back at the camp. The closer the Soviet army came, the more the bars filled, and the number of drunks increased.

One evening near the end, two drunken SS officers raped a woman from the town just off one of the dark roads leading from the town to Auschwitz. Colonel George Morgen, who was in charge of internal affairs for the SS, was sent to Oswiecim to investigate the alleged crime.

It was discovered during the investigation that the woman in question was a Jew. As Jews were without civil rights, the case was thrown out. It was not possible to rape a non-person. Privately, the two officers were sent to the eastern front for having violated the law prohibiting sexual relations between a German and a Jew.

Children's laughter in the parks grew thinner as their mothers' fear infected them. Expecting the crush of conflicting conquerers was anticipating the pain of the vise. In the most ironic way, there was safety in what they knew they had. A roof, coal, food, meager but food nevertheless, not being in *there*.

Was staying better than running? Would running place them, like rabbits, in the momentum of the signature chase and siege that ends most wars? With the most miniscule of personal power at their disposal, these decisions had to be made.

22.

It was with this in mind that Tyszka came to see Cecylia late one afternoon in her home where she lived with her mother, now overcome by dementia.

"I am afraid for you, Cecylia. Everything around here seems a bit crazy. Something different is in the air we breathe. Whatever it is has entered into us. It is upsetting the beat of our collective heart. Oswiecim breathes a certain way, and now it goes faster. It's as if the slow drumbeat I always feel inside the ways of our village has speeded up. There are more trucks and trains coming through to the camp.

"The crews are hardly permitted to rest before they must turn around and go back out for more Jews. I see them in the courtyard when Hoss has me come to illustrate him. He has me come often now, as if he is in a hurry. He talks much. And has me do his face in every way possible. With his uniform on, then off with it for common clothes. Cap on, cap off. A smile, then a frown as if he is in loathing. Then back to a smile again, or the hint of a smile. It's as if he doesn't know how he wants me to illustrate him."

Surprised by this unusual outburst, Cecylia only nodded.

"Lately, too, he sometimes tears up what I have done. When he does that, it is because I have forgotten to block what I see in his face and begin to show him as he is. Then I remember you and my father, and my responsibility and I begin to deceive myself and show him as he would like, and not the way he is. By this time, whenever he wants to see what I have done so far, the illustration is halfway between the little smile and a self-righteous smirk. This is when he gets mad and throws it away."

"I know everything is going faster," Cecylia said. "It is because the Russians are coming and no one knows what to expect. You must keep the commandant wanting you to perfect his likeness, the way he wants it. Just do not, as I have told you, do it too fast. Appeal to his vanity. Ask him to aspire to something great that will show up on your paper."

"That is hard for me. I see things when I am there. Last week, a few starved men ran from the line going to work toward the leftover piles of garbage near the kitchen. Most of them were shot. One of them managed to avoid the bullets and was pushing food into his mouth when the guards seized him. Hoss ordered them to hang him. When the man stopped kicking, they filled his open mouth with beans and left him there for all to see."

Cecylia tried to interrupt him, as she did not want to hear any more of this, but he could not get off the train of his own thoughts.

"I was lucky that day. Without realizing, I began to illustrate him as an ugly man, a monster began to show up on the paper. Good for me, he was called out of the office on an urgent matter, and I had a chance to hide the paper, as well as to begin a new face before he came back."

The afternoon sun was beginning to fade, and the room grew darker.

"The camp is going totally crazy. When I am in there, I hear screaming and sometimes crying. I think they are screaming out for me to help. I wish I could run to the children. Then *I* would scream at the guards, appeal to their reason to give the babies back to their mothers.

"At the same time, I must illustrate the commandant's face. And I hate him. I don't like what I feel. I have always been taught not to hate any person. That I could hate what a person does, yet not hate the one doing it. I used to think I could do that, as it is a nice idea. But when I see what he is responsible for doing, I cannot make the separation. I hate him. Not only what he does. No, I hate *him*."

Cecylia was afraid that he would not stop, ever. "Let me fix you a glass of tea," she said. Tyszka was so caught up in himself that he did not hear her.

"I am sad to tell you that it is becoming easy for me to hate. If what I have been taught is true, then it must apply to every man. It no longer makes any sense to me. The Nazi government hates what your people mean to them, and they also hate the people themselves? It is the thinking of the craziness that is upon me. If I could, I would destroy Hoss. If I could get my hands on the pistol he places on his desk, I would shoot him."

Cecylia continued to make the tea, accepting that Tyszka needed to say these things. She did not realize that he was finding his voice.

"But, I think I am only saying that. I wonder if I have the courage or whatever is necessary to pull the trigger. Oh, Cecylia, how I would like to do that. But I am afraid. I want to live. And I know they would kill me if I did that. I want to continue my art, love my friends, enjoy food, walking in the woods. Perhaps these are only excuses I make up in my head, just words. What I want is to stay alive.

"I am always hoping for the chance to know what else there is for me. I have read about other places, yet I have never been outside our village. I must see other places. There are people I have never met who one day will be my friends."

When he said this, he looked at Cecylia with a surge of love welling in him. What he wanted most was to be with her always. Although he was becoming more expressive with her, moments like this tested his ability to say what was in his heart. It was as if the most human tuning fork in his spirit was touched by the moment of her, and then resonated to his ability to wonder, and to the potential for satisfaction that was in him.

In the most fundamental way, Cecylia's presence, or even the thought of her, tapped into Tyszka's possibilites for generosity, for hope. Whenever this kind of moment came to him, he felt as if his chest was expanding with love. He was afraid that if he didn't let it out, he might explode with an assortment of feelings that could make her laugh if he tried to tell her. He realized that his sensibilities were expressed most effectively with a charcoal pen.

"It is obvious that something is happening. I have told you of the great numbers of trains and trucks coming to the camp. And when I look at the chimneys I see large billows of white and dark ashes blowing into the wind. I know what they are doing to Jews."

And then words began to slip out of his mouth, expressions without restrictions, yet so natural that even he wasn't surprised.

"Cecylia, if anything happened to you, then I would not want to live. Every now and then, when I am asked to illustrate a face, I get every detail of it just right, so that what I finish on the paper is the essence of the subject. It does not always happen. I come close a lot of the time, and I am proud of it, that I can come close. It is very complex."

Tyszka knew that the moment was now, even though it would be difficult for him to express his feelings which over his short life had been extremely self-contained.

"Cecylia, I love you," he blushed. He had never used the words before, and they felt odd. He realized they were some sort of declaration, a statement he chose to speak, one for which he did not have to apologize. Yet, somewhere in him he felt unworthy, even defensive and small, waiting, waiting for her response. If she took him lightly, he would think of himself as a child, such was the authority his infatuation had given to her. If she accepted him, he would assume the stature of someone elevated.

And if he should be touched by the wand of good chance, if she would just say, *I love you too,* he would be transformed on the spot into a man of worth.

As she began to answer him, Tyszka put his fingers to his lips, his way of asking her not to speak. It was as if his inner life was on the line at this moment. A distraction was needed, and he began to repeat himself.

"I want to first talk again about my work. I am greatly satisfied when I capture on paper the beauty of a person. That is why I am so good illustrating the baptism babies of the village. They are still true to themselves. There is nothing they do that is not them."

He was beginning to feel inadequate again. He was certain about his love for her, but did not how to express it.

"Let me try to explain," he said. In her own confusion, she was content to listen, and he seized upon that.

"I have just told you that I can sometimes get my illustrations just perfect. Mostly with babies, as they are what they are, nothing more, nothing less. And they are always beautiful.

"What I want to tell you is that it is different with you. What I really mean it is the same with you, except you are not a baby."

Shyness was beginning to knot his tongue. His best self was being muffled by a force he did not understand or control. Yet, he would not abide by it today. He knew that they were on the threshold of a crisis, that the usual equation that ruled lives was about to change. It was the time for him to say what was in his heart.

"When I look at you, Cecylia, when I am with you, I do not seem to care as much about things."

At this very moment, Tyszka's knotted tongue disappeared. He first put his head into his hands, then he held up an open palm as if to beseech her to be patient with him.

"I will try to tell you what I mean. Have you ever been with someone and you are so happy that you don't care about anything else? I mean not even about the sky if it was falling? Have you? Please tell me!"

"I have known such a moment."

"That is good to have happened to you. Perhaps now I will say more. Do you remember last year when you came into my church one day when I was praying? It was a Friday?"

"I remember."

"You wanted to ask me about this God I was praying to. You said to me, 'Who is this God?' and I did not know how to answer. I could not answer because I did not know. I still do not know." And then he said, "Really," as if to affirm his ignorance of deity.

"But I was bothered because it was you who asked me and I did not know. I have thought about it greatly since then.

"That is not what I wanted to tell you about that day. I wanted to tell you that when you came into the church then, and I saw you, it was as if there was a light in the aisle by the pew where I was kneeling. I know it sounds odd, but there was light coming from your skin. The dress you were wearing, it was green with lots of small flowers in it. Some were blue, some were yellow. The flowers also seemed to be alive with light.

"Ever since that day, whenever I see you I see the luster from inside you. I cannot help it. It happens with no one else. I am not crazy, nor am I confused," he said as an affirmation of himself with a boldness that was new for him.

"Please, please, Cecylia, don't say anything yet. Please. I am not done."

By now, she was sitting on her bed near him. When she did this, he got up and sat in the chair next to the bed. He was deep into himself, trying to say with words what he could best articulate in charcoal.

She would not comply with his request.

"Ever since you and I were playmates, Tyszka, I have known you to be such a dreamer. You could never stand to see anyone hurt. I don't know how many times you came to the rescue. Sometimes it was from the bully, sometimes just to give an extra pencil to someone in class who needed it. I have always admired that in you. You are a dreamer who does not limit himself to dreams. You have gone to the fence at night to bring vegetables to the prisoners."

Wanting to make certain to break the introspective spell he seemed to be under, she took a step toward him and looked him straight in the eyes.

"I often think about you, too," she said. "I admire you, what you do, the way you speak with people. The respect you have. I know that I am always glad when I am with you. We are such good friends. But I think about Kryztof sometimes and wonder where he is."

Her words broke the spell. "Yes, I do too," he responded. "Of course, I am annoyed that he is here in our conversation, but I am also concerned about him. I have a plan to find out about him, and I will tell you about it. But, first I must ask you if I am anything more to you than a good friend. I must know. I am beginning to lose a good feeling about the future."

He seemed to be afflicted suddenly with the unawareness that often accompanies self-preoccupation. His question about the depth of her feelings for him fell into the void for now, and was replaced quickly by the awful sights and sounds of the recent past.

"I will tell you what I saw at Auschwitz last week. A train came in when I was there. Hoss told me to come with him to the platform, to stop my work. When we got there, a tall man in a white doctor's coat began to wave a riding crop at the people getting off the train. He yelled 'links' and 'rechts,' some to the left, others to the right.

"Then he did something very odd. He yelled for everyone to stand still, even the guards. He began to pick out the old men who got off the train. After he dismissed the rest to the left or the right, he gathered the old men, about twenty of them, maybe twenty-five, and told them that he was going to conduct a race and they would be the runners. That they had to run from one end of the train to the other and back again. And that the first three to finish would be spared their lives and the rest sent to a gas chamber right away.

"He asked them, very slowly in Polish, if they understood him. That he would fire his pistol to start the race. They were tired and hungry. Confused, too. But they seemed to understand.

"They lined up to run. The tall doctor fired his pistol into the air, and they ran. It was sad to see them run. Have you ever watched an old person try to run? They are not capable. They creep, walk, run like toddlers. They try to run, walk a bit faster than a creep, but it is not a run. It is a herky-jerk on two legs."

Cecylia was beginning to get fidgety with this kind of talk.

"By the time they got to the end of the train to turn around, most of them were bent over, out of breath. It seemed like a long time before it was over. Of course, there were the three first to finish. I could see in them their youth, how they would have finished first even fifty years ago.

"They were panting, strangely sad winners. The rest were taken away. Then the most horrible thing happened. The doctor ordered the winners to come to him. When they did, he had them kneel down in front of him. He shot each of them in the back of the head.

"The most awful part was to watch the last of these three, seeing what was happening, trying to get on his feet. He was too weak. The doctor simply pushed him down on his face before finishing him."

By now, Tyszka's face was flushed with anger. If he were that old man fifty years younger, what he might do.

"I am ashamed for them. They were so deceived."

He hardly noticed when Cecylia put her hand on his shoulder.

"I am beginning to lose hope," he said again just as sharp and stunning noises from down the road interrupted their conversation. The crackle of gunshots mixed with heavy, yet delicate, sounds of glass breaking.

23.

Tyszka wished that he had brought his binoculars, although he did not need them to see what was happening. Gestapo armored cars were in the village rounding up the owners of small shops who had done business inside the gates of Auschwitz. The bread-makers, cobblers, barbers, carpenters, and repairmen who had worked in the SS quarters.

They had seen much. Too much. They were now being delivered to the consequences.

The abrupt turnaround from a mostly quiet hands-off policy to shootings and beatings in the streets was the revelation to those outside the camp that working with the Nazis did not make them free.

Dozens were being taken into the custody of death.

"Do you see, Cecylia? I was right. Something is going on. You must be extra careful, especially in town. I want you to stop going there. I will go shopping for you. Tell me what to get. I illustrate the commandant. I am not stupid, and so I know that as long as I am useful to him, I am safe."

"Do not worry, Tyszka. God will take care of us."

"You sometimes talk like a little girl," he said. "Like the third graders we once were. The God you asked me about that day in church, Cecylia, I do not know where he is. I speak with him every day. For a long time, I believed what they told me, that he is a loving God. But I see what goes on. If he is so loving, why does it go on?

"I ask him to be real to me, to say something so I know he is there. He says nothing I can hear. The best I can know that he might be there is when I see good people in the world. When I see my father who is always so kind. When I see the families of the baptism babies. They love each other. I see what they do. They think of the other person. They try so hard to get what their babies need."

The energy of his anger and sadness was growing so much that he could not stop talking.

"When I see these things, I want to think there must be a God who is so good that the leftovers of his goodness show up in some of these people. I think he must show up in you, Cecylia. I have never seen you being bad to anybody. You are considerate, even to the beggar in town. I have seen him, so dirty and smelly, ask you for a few zloty, and you give him what he asks. You respond to him. You ask him how he is."

She reached over to him and touched his face with the palm of her right hand. This time he noticed.

"Sometimes I am embarrassed when I see things like that. I think to myself, well, the good people are showing up God. They are more like God than God. And then I don't know what to think. I am full of shame because of these thoughts.

"I am so tired trying to figure it out. I ask him why he does not come into the camp, to stop the suffering and killing. I do not get an answer. So I say to him, 'What is this? A test to see if I believe?' Believe what, Cecylia? In a God who gives tests? What is in a test? Some pass, others fail. Why would a God want to give tests? It's seems silly to me. It has no merit. It is small-minded, not the mind of a God who is worthy of being a God. To give a test shows dependency. He is happy with those who pass, unhappy with those who do not. It seems that it does not take much to make him angry."

Cecylia had never heard him speak with so much intensity. His energy grew as he talked.

"I have said to him that he doesn't even tell us what he expects, except that we should love one another. That is a hard thing to do. I do not know how to love Commandant Hoss. He is wicked."

Tyszka now seemed to be talking to himself.

"I know, I know, I am told to hate the commandant's wickedness, but not him. So, am I expected to say to him at our next session, 'Commandant Hoss, I see the evil things you do to the Jews and other people here, and I think it is wicked. Please stop doing these things. But, I want you to know that I do not hate you. Only what you do. That I love you.'

"It would be easier for me to pick up his gun and shoot him than to say these things that are lies. They are lies because the only way I could get Hoss to stop doing wicked things is to kill him."

It was dark outside now, and Cecylia lit the lamp.

"You could say I should stop him from doing things, but I cannot except to kill him. I think this is not what I have been taught, but then how else could I stop him? There is no other way."

Tyszka knew that he was ranting, yet again he could not stop himself.

"You do not have to worry, Cecylia. I have already told you I could not kill him. Cecylia, you have loving ways about you. Do you ever think about this, that you automatically do what this God has said, to love one another? You just do this, as if it was impossible for you not to act this way. You have not even earned it that you are loving. I don't think so."

He began to mull over what he had just said, and the knot came back into his tongue. "I mean from what I have seen," he stammered." But I do not know for sure."

Cecylia was taken by Tyszka's straightforwardness.

"I do not think about such things, Tyszka. Please continue."

"Let us just say, because it is the way I think, that a person is a loving person, yet that person has not earned it. He is just that way. Is the God pleased with him? Or is he only pleased if the person has had to work at it, to be loving?"

He knew there was no certain answer.

"I want to think that God is pleased with the person who must make an effort. But then I say to myself, 'So what is special about an effort?' We think it means much, but perhaps a god does not think that way. Maybe it is only people who think this way, that an effort is good, I mean. You might say I am going in circles, ones that will never end. I would agree with that. I am fatigued in my soul with all of this. I do not have an answer. So, I am going to tell you what I have done to stop it all. I will tell you only if you are interested."

"Please tell me," she said, realizing that her own spirit was starved for such talk.

"One day I just said, 'God, I am not certain if you exist. I envy my friends who believe that you do. So, here is what I am going to do. I am making an announcement to you that you exist. I am doing this because I need you to exist. I do not know why. I am not afraid of you. I am not afraid of being punished. If you are a punishing god, you are needy and exacting, some things I do not see in a god. If you are this way, forget everything I am saying here because I would not want you in my life.

"I want you to be a personal god to me. I mean by this that when I would like to talk with you, that you hear me, that you are present to me. If what I think you must be, all powerful, all knowing, all present, is true, then you can do these things.

"If you can once in a while say something back to me, I would like that. Very much. But, I'm not looking for anything different, so you probably won't. And that is all right.'"

It was palpable that the agony of trying to find answers about God had been sucking the life out of his spirit, and that this singular declaration he had made, more to himself than to God, gave to the illustrator, at least for now, the freedom he needed to go on.

"I have said to him that he cares for me, Tyszka Dunajski, and for every other person. That he loves me beyond what I can imagine. That he is so naturally forgiving that, when I am bad, that he forgives me before the request breathes from my soul, and before the idea is born in my brain, or the words live on my tongue."

By now, he was so full of life that Cecylia saw him the way he always saw the baptism babies, innocent and beautiful. Tyszka was showing his own light.

"Cecylia, I'm sorry for carrying on so. Especially today when we all have so many concerns. I want to thank you for listening to me. I don't really have any great convictions yet about God. But since I talked to him this way, I have, at least, some ground to stand on. It is more than I ever had."

"I am happy for you," she said. "Happy in a way I have never felt before."

If he could have heard the words. For now, though, he could only hear himself.

"I still don't know what he wants from me," he continued. "Or, if he wants anything. I just don't know."

Before she could respond, he said, "I have a plan for Kryztof. First you must answer my question about us. If I am just a friend to you. You must know, too, that whatever your answer, I will pursue my plan for Kryztof because that is what you would want."

Cecylia looked at him as though she was her usual self, the one with the most quiet center Tyszka had ever known.

She was, though, right now in a swirl of inner disarray. She was beginning to see the unique mystery that was Tyszka.

She took his face into her hands, and said, "I do know that you always live in my heart."

24.

"I am going to be direct with Commandant Hoss. I will ask him if he knows about Kryztof and where he is. He must know because of what happened that night, and he always knows what is going on in the camp. I will ask him then to let him come back to Oswiecim, that what happened is my fault."

"There is danger in that for you, Tyszka, my . . . my dear friend." She did not know what to call him now. "If he knows you were the one bringing food, he might give you the consequences. You say yourself that he is a cruel man."

"You are right. He is. But he is vain and needs me for the illustrations. I can count on that."

Almost imperceptibly, they had begun to talk a bit lower about the plan. Soon, though, they could not hear each other. The noise in the streets was getting louder. Dogs barking, yelling, commands, metallic clanks and clangs— each and all together coming closer.

The epiphany is dark and startling when you know they have come for you. A kind of consummation of the countless moments of hope that we might be the exception to death's knock.

As soon as Tyszka heard the pounding on the door downstairs, he knew it was for Cecylia. Hoss needed him and knew how to get him when he wanted him.

"Fraulein Brydinski, open the door. Now, or we will break it down!" Upstairs, they instinctively hugged each other in fear, though Tyszka still new when he felt her hard and sinewy back that he was holding the one in whom he had invested his heart.

The impulse to ask her once again to breathe into his mouth, so he could know her forever, was struck dead by the booming sounds of rifle butts splintering the downstairs door.

An SS officer with drawn pistol led the race up the stairs, followed by five guards with rifles and bayonets, and ran into the room. The couple appeared like a statue frozen in a hug.

In that moment, Cecylia's rust-colored cat, Nutmeg, protector of his benevolent human, leaped across the room at the major's face. The officer smacked the cat hard to the floor, like a bee. Before Cecylia could help the stunned animal, the major grabbed it by the throat, held it at arms length against one of the windowless walls, and killed it with a single shot to the head.

"Jew cat," he shouted, dropping what remained of it on the floor. Cecylia, frozen in horror, put her hands to her mouth as if her incredulity could wipe the cat's blood from the wall and bed. The sound of the gun exploding in the tiny room seized up every nerve in her body. And the sight of the guards pointing their bayonets at her left her feeling dazed and removed, so that the scene appeared to be a nightmare dream.

The forceful grabbing of her elbows by two of the guards brought her back to her senses.

"Tyszka, help, help me," she screamed. Held tight by two of the guards, with a third thrusting his bayonet at him, he could do nothing as she was being shoved ahead to the floor below.

"I will help you. I will speak with Commandant Hoss about you. I promise you this," he yelled to her.

The major, pistol still in his hand, walked close to him. "So, you are the Tyszka we have been told not to harm. You don't look so special to me."

He turned to the two soldiers holding him, and asked, "Does he look special to you?" As they laughed, the officer spit into Tyszka's face. "This is to remind you that Commandant Hoss wishes to see you in his office at 4 pm It is now 2 o'clock. Do not be late."

25.

"It was a smart move for you to give us her name, Herr Doctor. It is good when we talk like gentlemen, like two professionals who understand what we each need. We have seen Dunajski with her in town. And we know that they visit each other in their bedrooms."

Suddenly, Hoss got more direct. "I think there must be something going on between them, going to the bedrooms. But, you told me that she is your girlfriend. Is she not?"

Although Hoss was singularly a man of brute power, he was cunning and manipulative when force did not meet his needs. He wanted the dentist alive, at least for now, because his relationship to the woman could help to keep Tyszka and his work chained to the commandant.

For weeks, he had been tweaking Penkalski about the girl, about how she would be better off in the women's camp at Birkenau than she would be in the clutches of the illustrator. He even insinuated that he could arrange for him to meet the girl periodically at his own house, now that his wife and family had gone back to Berlin.

When asked about his rival to the girl, the dentist had gladly given the commandant whatever information he needed, thinking that it would ensure Tyszka's doom. He told about the planning and the run to the fence, excusing his own behavior as simply the actions of a man trying to impress his woman. Surely Hoss, an amorous man, who had now taken up a Polish lover inside the camp, would understand that.

He tried in whatever ways he could to take advantage of his privileged position with the commandant. Sometimes, he would quote Dunajski as best he could, and when he could not remember, he would make things up.

"He has called you a crazy man, a murderer, someone who appears normal but is not. He has even told me that you are sometimes difficult to illustrate. That he cannot find any good in you."

He quickly noticed that the commandant would grimace whenever he told him that the illustrator vilified him as a man without nobility. It was clear to the dentist that Hoss saw himself, above all else, as a man of dignity who, with the highest honor, was doing the bidding of his Fuhrer.

Whenever Hoss would hear these things, his immediate thought was to arrest the illustrator and have him executed and burned. Yet, he was capable of unraveling the knit of his selfishness, to find whatever thread of cunning was good for him.

He quickly concluded that it was best to keep Tyszka happy, yet motivated. A man of his talents was not easy to find, and he could help the Third Reich, in his unwitting way, by illustrating an accurate picture of one of its heroes.

As for the dentist, Hoss would continue to dangle the captive girl in front of him as bait for a romantic fantasy that he might be allowed to see her.

"So, Herr Doctor, tell me about this girl we just took in. I saw her only once and could not help but notice that she is very pretty. What is her name again?" Of course, the commandant knew her name and everything else he needed to know about her.

"Her name is Cecylia Brydinski."

The reservoir of sadistic energy that fueled Hoss's ideas about Jews was, of course, available to him on a daily basis. It was like a storeroom of cruelty always available, always refilling itself without effort.

Occasionally, he would tap the hatred and meanness just because it gave him satisfaction.

"Do you miss seeing her?"

The question, a shot to the heart, was more of a revelation of Hoss's shallowness than a litmus test of Kryztof's yearning.

Yet, the loneliness that Kryztof began to feel when they first brought him to Auschwitz cut more deeply when Hoss asked questions about Cecylia's relationship to Tyszka.

Loneliness, a stripping away of human companionship, can leave a man spiritually nude if he does not have faith. As Kryztof never really had any, he was more than normally vulnerable in Auschwitz.

Even as he increasingly engaged in the pettiness of camp life, the never ending negotiations—two potatoes for a speck of soap, four cigarettes for the bottom scoop in the deep pot of morning soup where the meager vegetables and meat festered—he began to feel a loss of his self-respect. If regard for oneself is a daily installment against loneliness, Kryztof was beginning to forfeit it by the hour.

The barrack he was quartered in was less than adequate, even when compared to the sordid conditions of the regular prisoners. He slept two across, rather than the usual three, in three tiers of plain wood, each covered by a one inch cloth mattresses stuffed with straw.

His food was inadequate. An unsweetened cold coffee substitute in the morning. A metal bowl of watery soup with potatoes and leaves for lunch. Stale bread and water for dinner. He was becoming exhausted.

As a dentist, he had become used to certain privileges of the professional class. There was respect, and he could come and go as he pleased. Yet, here in the camp the only sense of privilege he had was the reprieve from death, and that only for a while. He and the *Sonderkommandos*, who took care of the work of the crematoriums, knew that they lived only as long as they were useful and efficient in their work.

They knew, too, that most were gassed whenever the Waffen SS thought they knew too much about the system of killing or about individual Nazis who ran the operation. The matter of time began to hang heavily over Kryztof's head, ironically, at the same time as the worst of all possible changes was occurring in him.

He was beginning to lose his individuality. He began to see himself as the same as every other man in the barrack, a useful cog in a machine he loathed. In fact, he was filled with a natural hatred of it. Although this was so, each day ground him into the same shape as the man next to him.

At first, he was even lonesome for his status as a man, as someone to be regarded just because he was a man. He was beginning, though, to lose even the desire for his adulthood. It was too difficult to maintain, and in certain ways he was satisfied to be like a child.

Becoming dependent was not all that bad, he rationalized. He no longer had to make many decisions, when to go, when to come, when to get up, go to bed, eat, to defecate. That was done in the morning. The body must adjust to the system. At least he had a full minute to relieve himself, double the time allotted to the regular prisoners.

Yet, in a slow, creeping sort of way, he was losing his sense of himself. The prisoners chosen by the SS Death's Head units to be leaders in the blocks were usually over-reactive types, often cruel. Staying out of their way by yielding to their wishes was turning Kryztof into a bootlicker of sorts, though he still had the ability to monitor his motives and observe his actions. He knew that when this ability ended, that the moist core of his humanity would dry up, reduced to a working part that eats, sleeps, defecates, and works. That he would no longer be Dr. Krystof Penkalski. He would be number 011653.

He missed Cecylia. Most of the time, though, no more than he missed a cup of real coffee in the morning, or going and coming as he pleased. It was not that he did not feel drawn to her when the occasion beckoned. He just had little idea what was expected beyond that. Several times he had seen love expressed exquisitely. Once in a restaurant he noticed an older couple entirely wrapped in each other's conversation. They went together in a jazzy ensemble of speaking and listening. And they sparkled.

Before he could ever get to that place with Cecylia, he would first have to forgive himself for trading her freedom for a promise to see her again. He wondered if it was possible to get redemption after betraying another's welfare. He would have to find a way.

26.

His secretary was not certain if she had understood his directions, that Tyszka was to be brought in when the dentist was still in his office. Timidly, she knocked. With a smile spawned by the anticipation of cruel amusement, Hoss opened the door.

"Welcome, Herr Dunajski. I believe you know the dentist."

Tyszka's initial shock to see Penkalski here in the commandant's office was quickly replaced by confusion. Although he was glad to see an acquaintance, he felt a greater joy yesterday in the wish that a part of the ashes he saw hanging over the village would be all that remained of the dentist. Unsure, he looked at Hoss before putting out his hand as if it was a chip of iron expecting to be pulled in by the magnet of good manners.

The dentist shook his hand, not sure if the illustrator knew that he had succumbed to loneliness, and clung to petty privilege by turning Cecilia over to the authorities. His impulse to hide was immediately verified as the commandant began to play the earnest sadist.

"And you both know the woman, Cecylia—how do you say, Breadski?"

Tyszka answered. "Yes, we know her, and she is Brydinski," spelling out each letter of her name. The anger

143

in his tone surprised Hoss, triggering displeasure and bluntness in the man used to deference.

"I want to know whose girlfriend she is. Tell me now."

Smitten by the inference that it could be he, the dentist knew only that his loneliness immediately took on a different color. It was as if the dark night of his soul was being infused with a bold light that allowed him to see shadows.

"She is *my* girlfriend," the dentist answered.

The rules of this kind of exchange were not difficult for either of the prisoners to understand. In dealing with a cruel and alcoholic father, Penkalski the boy had developed strategies for survival. When to reveal, when to hide, when to talk, and to be quiet.

The poverty of a subsistence plot of land had taught young Tyszka about the nuances of pitching a deal on home-grown potatoes and vegetables. They both knew that with Hoss in charge certain outcomes were expected in a game of words. They both knew that here words were the utterance of egos, an expression of right and wrong. And that when these clashed for supremacy in the camp the stakes could become extreme. Whatever rules there were applied only to prisoners, and the most ironic one was that winners became losers.

It was always difficult to know what Hoss was up to in a sparring session of this sort. Who knew what trap a question was setting? Tyszka admired Kryztof's quick answer. It had a certain recklessness to it.

"So, she is your girlfriend. Do you agree, Herr Dunajski?"

"Yes, she is his girlfriend," he answered. He would not be caught in the lure of questions designed to disparage, and calculated to effect humiliation in both men.

He calculated, too, that the line of questions was irrelevant to the essential issue, survival. For himself as well as for Cecylia. He thought for a moment that he might even like Penkalski.

"Herr Commandant, if I may speak for a moment," he pleaded.

"Of course, go ahead," he said in an affected tone that only the powerful who are trying to pretend equality know.

"Of course, you know that Cecylia was taken prisoner yesterday. I want to know if she is well. And where she is. And could you, would you, let her go. She has done nothing wrong."

This was favored territory for Hoss. He was the rich man being asked for a handout, the executioner with portfolio.

"It is preposterous."

"It is an opportunity. For you to do something great, something you do not have to do, yet you do simply because you can. It is the sign of a great man," Tyszka replied.

His response annoyed Hoss. "Do not patronize me. Do you not know why I have asked you to come here? Why I ask you to illustrate my face?"

He started the rant in a low, guttural tone, a sign that he might be losing his ability to sustain the fellowship he liked to pretend when he was with Tyszka.

"For months I asked who was the best person to prepare the world to see my face in the history books. Photographs will not do justice to my face. Only the person whose craft matches the brilliance of his art will do."

He was getting louder, his face flushed.

"You ask me now to do something you call great. How can you be an artist if you cannot see?"

As was his habit when he was feeling the excitement of his anger growing, he drew close to the object of his wrath. Then he stepped back and began to pick at his fingernails. Finally, with booming voice and face in Tyszka's face, he shouted, "See the Jews I kill each day. See what is left of their filthy selves in the smoke. Nothing is left. They are gone. I am meticulous. I keep records. When this work is over, the world will know that I have killed over two million Jews here in Auschwitz and Birkenau. Two million, do you hear? Two million." He liked the ring of numbers and repeated them over and over.

"I do not have to do anything more to prove my greatness. And you ask me to free one Jew and call that great. Himmler has warned us that we might be soft, that we will each want our one Jew. Well, here you are asking me if Cecylia will be my 'one Jew.' We play no more today. She will be my one Jew only as long as you stay here in Oswiecim and prepare me for the history books. The people will want to know about me, the man who freed the world of Jews. Do you understand me?" he shouted.

Tyszka began to feel dizzy. Too much to bear. Surreal. He was listening to a fanatic. Free, yet a prisoner. In love with a woman held hostage to his talent, to his willingness to compromise. The wrong word might bring death.

He thought about saying the wrong word, to bring this burden to an end.

He had only to say what he was thinking, "*You are not great, you are small, vicious and evil. If I could, I would shoot you in your hideous face right now.*"

He thought again about Cecylia's reminder to him that he must always think of his father and his friends whenever he felt, in her words, "like being irresponsible."

"Yes, please, then, keep her safe. I promise I will continue to illustrate."

"Now, we are getting somewhere. Another man who knows how to get things done."

With the carelessness of an ideologue who spins repetitive ideas, Hoss continued, abruptly, "You are now both cooperating with the historic progress of the Third Reich." Then he simply said, "I will remember this."

He had established the momentary balance that he wanted with each of the men. By cooperating with Hoss, the dentist thought his woman was safe from Tyszka who would provide for the woman's safety by cooperating with Hoss.

Almost immediately, though, Hoss tipped the scales again. It was his way to keep them off guard about their security, as well as on guard about him. He enjoyed it that way.

"Herr Dunajski, do you know that your friend here, the dentist, turned his beloved Cecylia over to the authorities?

He has told us about the ways she helped you and him deliver food to the Jews."

The revelation hit Tyszka as if double punched. Hoss knew about his deliveries under the camp fence, and Kryztof had turned in his beloved Cecylia.

A more belligerent man might have rushed across the room to grab Penkalski by the throat. Whether by temperament or the introjection of his gentle parents' ways, he did not.

Instead, he decided to accept this revelation that he could do nothing about, that Hoss knew of his complicity in delivering food to the prisoners, an offense punishable by death.

"Why did you not take me prisoner when you first knew?"

"Come, come. You artistic types are all alike. You do not know how to make the deal, get what you want. You are so caught up in your ways that you starve for your work. You, Dunajski, you are an idealist. I can see it in you. How you talk, the way you illustrate. At first, I would be angry with you for taking so much of my time. But, then as I watched you, I began to understand your quest for perfection. I like that. It reminds me of the demands I make on my own efficiency. It is the way I run this camp.

"I think, perhaps, I too am an idealist. You want your work to reach the highest standards. Just like me. I know that the German people are the purest people. Our ancestors are the Aryans. We are born to greatness, and it is the Jews and the beggars who will try to take this away from us.

Our Fuhrer says we must get them before they get us. I get them. It is my highest goal, my own idealism."

If not for Tyszka's intrusion, he was like a freshly wound clock, ready to tick on a spring fully loaded.

"I am sorry to interrupt, Herr Commandant, but I do not know why this stopped you from arresting me. Please."

The delivery of a delusion manifests itself in many ways, some odd, others normal. Given his power as camp commandant, it was easy for Hoss to think of himself as intrinsically superior to each of the prisoners in his camp. As no one would dare to challenge his words, he increasingly failed to distinguish between leverage of intellect and lust for power, often twisting them together into a single justification for his actions.

"I think it is a better way to keep you free." As he stepped closer, he looked directly into Tyszka's eyes, before saying, "And that is how it will be."

Perhaps it was the intimidating way that Hoss stared at him that made Tyszka look away. Or perhaps he was again walking the thin line that separates what is and what ought to be. He could argue and lose, or wait for another day.

Turning to the dentist, Tyszka asked if it was true about Cecylia.

"It is true," said the dentist. "But only in a way."

"It is true or it is not true," Tyzska replied with an intensity that filled up the room.

The exchange was interrupted by an urgent knocking at the door. Hoss knew the knock and immediately opened the door. It was Kramer. "Herr Commandant, we have an urgent matter that needs your attention." Hoss picked up his cap and pistol, and left, leaving the two men alone.

After an uncomfortable moment of silence, Penkalski answered. "I have been lonely for her. I will have a chance to see her, I was told. I will make it worth her while. I will," though he had the look of a child discovered committing an original sin.

"Please, Tyszka, she must never know. Promise me you will keep it a secret. Always a secret. I am doing what is best for her."

Though it was not in his nature, Tyszka felt only scorn. He would not, though, hurt Cecylia by telling her what the dentist had done. She did not need to be hurt any further, especially now that she was a prisoner. She might need her illusions.

27.

She had already been tattooed the night before she woke up in the women's camp at Birkenau, a short walk from Auschwitz. Her wooden bed, the lowest of three tiers, was where newcomers had to bunk. The top tier was reserved for women with the most camp time. No one could splatter the watery feces of diarrhea upon them in the night. The lowest was for the least in seniority, as well as the end point of body fluids from everyone above.

If a nightmare exists only in the imagination, this was more dreadful because it was real. The lights in her bunk-house, a stable designed for horses, came on at 4:00 am when female orderlies stormed in flailing reedy whips, yelling "Out, Out." It did not take long to know that it was better to jump from the wood than to be hit by the long semi-flexible whip that left a wound, sometimes bloody, on the thighs or buttocks.

Each woman had no more than one half minute for her personal toilet needs. Then the thin mattresses were squared off, and the equally thin blankets had to cover each section neatly.

Like most inmates, Cecylia was left only with a pin-striped shirt and pants, even though it was late winter. They were forbidden to wear the bed blanket around their shoulders when they took the two-mile walk to work at the

I.G. Farben factory in Monowitz where artificial rubber and synthetic gasoline were manufactured.

Her first breakfast was a thin soup and cold coffee. Fortunately, she had made several friends quickly. Anna, a number to the Nazis, was a bright and well-read hairdresser in Krakow before her imprisonment. They met in the camp barbershop where Anna's job was to shave off the hair of each new prisoner.

"They are trying to debase you, and use me as the debasing machine. Any fool could do what I do, but I'll take it. It is easy work and keeps me alive. You seem like a nice person," she said in the understated way strangers make overtures of friendship. "When all of your hair is cut off, you will look older. And then they might not want you to work in the factory. They will send you to the gas chambers. I know you do not look old, but here a person can get old fast."

She left just enough hair on Cecylia's head to afford her a healthier look about her face, today still as fresh and pretty as it was often beheld by Kryztof and Tyszka.

"Now, if they clear your block to make a selection of those who will continue to work and those who will die, they call it a special treatment, you will look better than the others. Remember also to always rub your cheeks hard so you will look like the health is running in your face."

In a gush of genuine friendship, she continued.

"I will tell you other things to do. I have survived for more than two years, so I know. I do my work, so you see how they leave me alone."

Cecylia nodded her head, as if she understood.

"Do not look at what they do to the children. Never. If you do, you will fold into yourself and die. It is too cruel. Forget about justice. There is no justice here. We all have come into this world from the same profound emptiness, we are something from nothing. But we came as Jews. You do not deserve what is happening to you. If you did deserve it, you would find the strength to endure.

"But, when you think there is an injustice happening here and you think too much about this, you will want justice. When it does not come, you will grow disappointed and weak. And you will die. You must accept life in Birkenau as a universe without justice, and then you might survive."

Anna stopped cutting the hair in snippets, a useful way to create time for talking, before suddenly taking a large snatch of Cecylia's locks and deftly sculpting it between the long edges of the scissor blades. The rasping feel of the quick, grinding cut caused Cecylia to look up. Satisfied that she had achieved the desired effect, Anna asked emphatically, "Do you understand what I am telling you?"

"I think I do," she responded.

"You must try to find limits. This will keep you sane. I discovered this one day when they made me throw the bodies of gassed women into the pits of fire. The stoves could not handle them all. I became sick helping to pick up their nude bodies and tossing them into the flames. I had to throw up. I noticed that if I looked at one of the dead people, it helped. I saw a beautiful girl, about twenty-five years old, whose body had fallen a bit separate from the rest. Her eyes were open and I thought she was staring at me. This helped me to see her as a person again. It helped me to create limits out of chaos in my mind."

For her own sake now, she stopped and walked a few steps to the sharpener where she angled the scissor blades on a pumice wheel. She watched it spin sparks before resuming her lecture.

"Pay attention to the little things. Wash your underwear with the smelly herbs you'll see on the side of the road you walk to work. There is a sign in the washrooms that says 'After shitting, wash your hands.' Do it. It is good against typhus, and it is good because the Germans are watching. They pay attention to details."

Before Cecylia could thank her, she said, "One more thing. Keep your eyes open for fleas. Never let one get near you. Check your blanket before you go to bed. And your mattress. They like to live in these things. Never let them bite you. You can get sick with a headache. Then it gets worse. You can get a fever and begin to imagine seeing things that are not there. I have seen this with my own eyes. Last week a woman, not much older than you, died from the disease. She got sick and depressed from it. When she went into the hospital, we knew she was dead. Once you are too weak to work, they will let you die."

Cecylia wanted her to stop. It was too much, too fast. But the intensity of Anna's desire to be helpful would not allow it.

"A woman who works in the hospital unit has told us that sometimes the doctor in charge sticks a long needle into the heart to kill such a person. They do not then have to bother any more.

"When a block is infected with the typhus from the fleas, the doctors clear out everyone before fumigating the block. Then, almost without exception, they send everyone from there to the gas chambers so that new prisoners can use the block.

"The same woman I told you about who works in the infirmary has told us that the doctors speak together about how they are saving people from the typhus by doing this, how they are providing a great therapy."

The sharp whistle blew. Time to line up outside to be counted. Over and over before going to Monowitz for the day. Driven work. A little soup, maybe part of a potato. A brief conversation with others bound only by circumstance, the exhausting walk back to emptiness.

The hardship of the first days became the enduring background for Cecylia. It was a dread that later became almost customary in its repetition. Soon, she came to know the strange terror that is a mixture of confusion, fright, and disbelief.

One of the older women who had slipped by the wand of death selection when she first arrived, or was spared by a whimsical display of merciful omnipotence, had struggled on the walk back to camp. She was exhausted in mind and body.

As they entered the camp, Cecylia thought she heard music. Not loudspeaker music that was sometimes played. This music was resilient and pure, without intermediary, direct from the strings and reeds of instruments being played right then.

Now she saw them. There must have been fifteen or sixteen women prisoners, playing as if to welcome them home. Cecylia recognized the song, an old and popular Polish street song played by itinerant musicians. Many of the women here had learned the song in childhood, which seemed a long time ago.

Just then the exhausted woman began to run in spastic circles. She would fall in the dirt, get up and run again, all the while screaming for something to eat. "I need food, please, anyone, give me food. I must eat."

No one knew what to do. This went on for a few minutes while everyone watched before an SS officer ran across the courtyard, Luger in his hand. It was Hoss's adjutant, Kramer, thought by the inmates to be inflexible and unimaginative.

He stood over the frantic woman and fired two shots into the air. All was quiet as she began to tear out tufts of her hair where she spun in the wet of her own urine. Cecylia ran to help her.

"Please, sir, help her. Let me help her," she pleaded to Kramer.

"Stay away from her!" he shouted.

As she knelt by the deranged woman's side, Cecylia flashed back to a similar overcast day in Oswiecim when she was a child. One of the neighborhood dogs, on a walk with his master, had suddenly gone mad, and was running in circles, frothing at the mouth. Soon, a policeman came and instructed the small group of people watching to back away. He grabbed the dog's leash to hold it at arm's length. Then he shot it in the side. She remembered how the poor creature lurched and fell over.

As she watched the top of the woman's head matting with blood from pulling out her hair, Cecilia began to feel faint. And odd. Again, everything was happening too fast. She was starting to lose her grip. Today was beginning to weave into the knit of the past, and she was not sure if she knew the difference anymore. The dog was here, today. No, there, years ago. Maybe here *and* there. Did the policeman shoot a woman back then? Could he shoot her today? Yes, he could. Maybe he would.

She was beginning to think that she was in two places at the same time. For a moment, three places. Shot dog, crazy lady, incinerator smoke.

Life was turning its back on the order and sense that she willed to direct her life ever since her father died when she was a teenager. She was conscious, though, that these were her thoughts. This awareness became the thin connection to the reality of what was happening to her today.

Enough, she said to herself. Cecilia stood up from the woman's side, and directed her own heart to stop thumping in her chest. Then, firmly and with as much dignity as she could muster, she said a most unusual thing to Kramer.

"Shoot her!"

Finishing off the desperate woman would not be enough for Kramer whose instincts for cruelty today belied his reputation for being dull. He seized the moment of the woman's disintegration as if it were a thing to spin, not knowing or caring where or when it might stop.

He looked at Cecylia for a second or two before responding to her request. "There are no mercy shots for Jews. We are running short of bullets and they are too valuable to waste."

The adjutant yelled for everyone to go to their barracks immediately. They did. And the band resumed playing an old Klezmer street song called, "That's How We Live Every Day."

28.

It was only later that night when the order for *lights out* sent her to bed that Cecylia's body began to calm down, though she realized that the day had forever marked her.

She found it curious that she began to think about Tyszka in ways that she never before had. She was not simply lost in thought about him this night when she was so alone. It was as if he was physically present in the thoughts, closer to her than she had ever felt before.

Whatever it was that made him Tyszka seemed to be wrapped around her body as a warm and protective cover, and seemed to enter into the bones of her body, and into her spirit before mingling, if only for an instant, with her entire being as if they were one person. Perhaps it is possible to call forth the spirit of someone we love to the core, so that a part of the indivisible comes to us, not like a thin voice, but like a presence that can shake us to shivering. Although she did not know if this could happen, the last thought she remembered before falling asleep was that, from a distance, she had breathed him into herself.

At the same time that she was thinking of him, Tyszka also began to feel odd, as if he was being seized without warning by a majestic breath leaving him, but through a gauze that made it difficult for him to exhale. At first, a stillness lined his inner skin, and in the quiet he thought he heard eerie shouts and soft whispers.

Tyszka arrived five minutes before his appointed time. Hoss presented a peculiar appearance, sitting in the usual chair for posing in his full-dress uniform, but with his bare feet soaking in a long, shallow pot of water.

"My feet sometimes feel as if they are burning. I need the cold water to soothe them. They will not get in the way. Just ignore them. Before you start, let me tell you that I have not been satisfied with your work. Do you sometimes notice late at night that if you listen carefully you can hear the sounds of big guns in the distance? The war is coming closer to us."

The commandant began to pick at his nails, one of the signs Tyszka understood to indicate that Hoss's temper was beginning to boil.

"The Fuhrer has ordered us to speed up our work. If we must move to the west I want the completed portraits. I want you to work faster, more efficiently. Do not make so many mistakes. I am impatient with the way you have been erasing and starting over again."

He picked one of his feet from the pot. "Sometimes, it is too cold," he said.

Tyszka wanted to ask him about Cecylia again, but he knew that this minute was not the right one.

"Please, Commandant, sit still."

As usual, he thought he should start with the most innocuous part of Hoss's face. He would go to the bottom of the egg-shape, to the chin, which was small and unremarkable, not difficult to sketch. Or so he thought. At first, its smallness conveyed little to Tyszka, until he noticed that its distance from Hoss's lips was shorter than usual, setting up an unusual juxtaposition. His lips, too, were thin.

The insufficient distance, thin lips and tiny chin, each insignificant by itself, came together for the illustrator as a triptych of pouts. If he drew what he saw, the Commandant would not like it.

Yet, before going any further, a curiosity about his gift welled up inside Tyszka.

"Commandant Hoss, if I may, only to help me, I would like to ask you a question."

"Go ahead, but get on with it."

"I want to know how you feel today."

Instead of the reprimand Tyszka half-expected for asking a personal question, Hoss stood, both feet in the bucket of water and, as if singing a song of exaltation, shouted, "I am so glad that someone notices and wants to know."

Taking his right foot out of the bucket, he stomped it, like a sullen child, on the floor before he said, *Meine nerven sind vollkommen zur grunde gegangen.*

"I am sorry, Herr Commandant, I know only a little German."

"I am saying to you that my nerves are totally shot."

He sat down and began to dry his feet with a small white towel.

"You know how hard I work here. I have great responsibilities, especially now when things are heating up. We have orders from Berlin to go faster with the work. Yet, no one seems to notice the hard work. It is expected. So, do I answer your question?"

"Yes, you answer my question."

Once again, with these words Hoss was, ironically, confirming Tyszka's gifts for seeing into others. Although it might get him through the present crisis of interpretation, he could not deny the gift. He could only misuse it.

Without hesitation, he decided to misuse his talent by sketching the triptych into an integration of the parts so that the lower section of Hoss's face appeared mildly handsome. Tyszka effected this by imperceptibly increasing the distance between chin and lips which he made slightly fuller and less pursed.

This alteration of the truth switched the image of the bottom part of his face from a slight grim puckering to a beckoning, as if he were saying, "Come, walk in the sunlight with me."

Tyszka was beginning to feel a nausea of the soul. He had taken the truth and distorted it. He did not know why it was necessary for him to observe and honor the truth. He did not work at speaking and acting as if he was trying to conform to it. Or even to reflect it. Most of the time, it simply happened with him, although he noticed that sometimes he tended to exaggerate in small ways when he spoke about himself. A single sale of a portrait became two, a two-mile walk became three in the telling.

Yet, he would get fatigued when he overstated and sometimes, to counter this tendency, he would commit himself for a day to speak words that exactly reflected the experience of his life and how he perceived it, trying, almost desperately, to say only the truth. For him truth, under or over-stated, was a lie.

And he was afraid to live a lie, not so much because this violated his morals, but because it tainted his gift. He knew that he must live his gift for it to stay intact. He also knew that his innocence was leaving him, that the manipulations he planned against Hoss to take advantage of his vanity were tainting his ability to see clearly—the essence of the gift. In small, but meaningful, ways in the past few months he had already desecrated the expectations that grew from the roots of his idealism. He had, in fact, prepared himself in incremental and acceptable ways for what he was about to do.

One look into Hoss's eyes told Tyszka that he could not portray him as he was, dishonest, corrupt, unprincipled. If one could be evil-minded, Hoss was evil-eyed. His eyes did not appear to be able to receive the spirit of another, did not reflect respect.

Sometimes, when Tyszka looked straight at him, the commandant would drop his head slightly to the right, an unusual way for a man of excessive pride to hold himself. In doing this, the pupils of his eyes involuntarily moved up and to the left in their sockets so he could look back at the illustrator.

Coupled with Tyszka's pretentious depiction of Hoss's mouth and lips, that look, when he made it, was incongruous. The work of bridging good and evil would be too much for the nose, he thought. He must fashion a sparkle in the dullness of the eyes.

He would turn the eyes back down to a normal position, and sketch in lively pupils with one stroke in the center of each iris. Deep in reflection, Tyszka wished mightily that he could, like a god, actually limn the light of love into every man.

29.

He had overdone it. In place of a face whose eyes had been dulled by a soul rotting in hatred, Tyszka sketched Hoss with perfectly symmetrical eyes. Where once there was a void, there now was a light that would insinuate a human connection to others.

It was too much for the illustrator. He would have to take something from the radiance. If he did not, the complete compromise would undo him. He decided, with deft strokes of his charcoal pen, to remove light from Hoss's eyes, a fitting trade-off, he thought, as he was afraid of losing his own. It was also necessary to buy time for himself and for Cecylia. He must make Hoss displeased with the portrait.

The artistry of his craft would be put to a new test. Ironically, he would have to create a flaw in the lie. This was strange territory for a man whose signature pieces always amazed subjects and their friends. "Yes, this is Kazimier," and "How like my Regina this is," they would say. Fidelity was the most beloved quality of Tyszka's work.

Now, after his manipulations of Hoss's mouth and eyes, he must look at his craft in a different way. He must ask it to delete deceit on top of a lie.

He tried. Again, he tried. And again, until he realized that it could not be done this way. He must first erase the lie and replace it with deceit. And then hope that Hoss would be dissatisfied.

By now the half-hour he was allotted was almost up. He must complete what he was doing, and he must also ask about Cecylia.

"Herr Commandant, please tell me how the dentist is, and his girlfriend, Cecylia. I wonder if she is well."

"How do I know? I run this whole camp, and you think I am concerned about one person. They are all the same to me. Yes, I have read that you artistic types think everyone is unique as a snowflake. They are all Jews. Would you pick out one vermin over another and care about it?" he asked.

Tyszka did not dare respond, as he might lose control of himself and say what was on his mind.

Nor did Hoss want to agitate the illustrator whose best work, he thought, was done while he was calm.

"Stop!" Hoss got up and walked barefooted to the door of his office. "Have Kramer come in here immediately," he shouted to his secretary.

"While we are waiting to see how she is—Kramer will explain—we have been told by some of my men that there has been a stirring among the inmates both here and at Birkenau. Nothing they can identify. A stirring nevertheless. I cannot expect you to know anything about it, but I am sure some of the inmates do. Sometimes, these things amount to nothing. A rumor, a wild story, starts to buzz around the camps like a bee and everyone begins to get agitated. Usually, it is nothing."

Kramer knocked at the door.

"Come in."

"Herr Commandant, you wanted to see me?"

"Yes, I want to know how our friend's girlfriend, or should I say 'female friend,' is doing. What is her full name, Mr. Dunajski?"

"Cecylia Brydinski."

"She is good. We are keeping our eye on her, as you have ordered. We have assigned her to work at Monowitz where the conditions inside the factory are good. She is good."

"Make sure she has enough food. I do not want her to get tired like the others. That is all."

Kramer saluted, spun, and left.

"You see how I take care of her."

"I am grateful that you take care of her."

"Let me see what you have done so far." He went to the table where the illustrator had put the unfinished work of the day, and picked it up to examine it.

The edginess that Hoss felt since receiving orders from Berlin to increase the daily death count was evident.

"The chin and lips, superb. But the eyes are only good, not great. There is something missing in them." Attempting humor, he added, "Where is my nose? Am I to be a man without one? Will they say in the history books, under your portraits of me, 'Lieutenant Colonel Hoss, the Man Without a Nose'?" His try at being funny was strained.

"I do not think they will say that."

"What, then, do you think they will say?"

He was calculating, as was his way, to make Tyszka squirm.

"I think they will say things about you that will make you well-known."

The commandant looked at him. Tyszka noticed that he was squinting with a contempt that, ironically, seemed tinged with respect.

"You are good at sparring. A unique style. You never force it."

Tyszka did not know what to say.

"Have you studied karate?"

Suddenly, he was afraid that he might laugh at the question, which seemed, in the context of the observation, tired and obvious. Instead, he feigned excessive respect.

"No, sir, I am flattered, but I have never."

"You take the force of an attempted blow and use it against your opponent. You are good at this. Your dentist friend is good, too, but not as good as you."

He did not like being compared to Penkalski.

"Herr Commandant, I have not had time to get to your nose. I am trying very hard to make my sketches of you convey your discipline and your accomplishments. It takes time."

"I do not have the time. What is missing in the eyes? The eyes of a great man must show his vision. I do not see vision in the eyes."

It was the reaction that Tyszka had effected. Deleting light from the commandant's eyes left the paper image as incomplete as Hoss's own character.

Tyszka begged the commandant for time to get to know him as a subject.

"Sometimes, when I do not sketch with satisfaction, it is not because of what is missing in the one I am trying to represent. It is because there is something missing in me. What is usually absent is my knowledge of the person."

"Do not tell me again that I must aspire to something great and noble. It is a stupid thing to say. Everyone here knows I am already these things. Now. Today."

"Commandant, I know this is true. I can see how you run this camp. That you are busy. If you would allow me for a few days to go about the camp, and Birkenau, I will talk with your men, with the prisoners you could have condemned. You have allowed them to work for the greater good of Germany. They will know your greatness, and I will sketch it."

Hoss paused, yet only slightly.

"I have said that you are good with your kit and with your words. I know that. Now I see again that you think I am stupid."

Fear seized Tyszka. He had heard the stories about Hoss and the rage.

Instead, Hoss continued calmly, ever the pragmatist. "I am disappointed that you see how I run the camp, and yet you do not see the greatness. But, I am told that your type needs reassurances. Perhaps you do see, and you are so faint-hearted about your own self that you are incapable of grasping the grand significance of what you see.

"I will give you one week with a special pass and entry letter that will explain your business. Talk to anyone you want about me. It will be good. I am busy and do not want to see you again until after your interviews.

"I will warn you, though. When I send for you again, you are to sit with me and do a completed illustration of me, just as I am. You have a reputation for accuracy. If you do not depict me as I am, you will pay the consequences."

Almost majestic in full uniform, he moved into Tyszka's face and, with the imperious tone of the sanctimonious, said, "Do you understand me?"

"I do."

"Good. Go now. The letter will be brought to you tomorrow."

Tyszka knew that the letter would give him access to Cecylia and to the camp. To heaven and to hell.

30.

By any standard, Mietek Kerner's right hand was disproportionately large. He also made it lethal by the tiny metal ring, fashioned from a spoon he traded for two potatoes, that he sometimes wore on his pinky finger. Whenever he gave a direct order, the *Sonderkommandos* who worked in the crematorium preferred to snap to the performance of their duties rather than to submit to the pain meted out by his oversized hand.

It was a simple ring, easy to hide, that he used to carry out threats unheeded. Its small crown of jagged metal could puncture the flesh of upper arms, enough to cause pain and draw a little blood, but not enough to incapacitate. To make a point, he would sometimes practice on the corpses of his fellow Jews waiting to be put on the elevators that went upstairs to the furnaces. Their newly gassed bodies would squirt blood. And when a worker, exhausted and sunken into his skeleton, was sent to the gas chamber, Kerner would take the ring from his pocket, put it on and, in front of the men, stab what little was left of an upper arm where the ring would bite into bone.

Sometimes, when he did this he would have to work at extricating the ring from a corpse who seemed to be hanging on to him, as if for dear life. Kerner seemed delighted when this occurred, as he thought it made the consequences of his threats clear. "I hope you get the point," he would say, and each time howl with mad laughter at his own perceived wit.

He wore a green triangle patch on his prison uniform. One really did not need to know it identified him as a criminal, as he wore the scowl of the maniac. He had once thrown a grandmother he was robbing to her death from a third floor window, after he had raped her.

Kryztof first met him in one of the outer rooms of the gas chamber where the nude dead bodies were dragged or carted for the dentist to extract gold from their teeth. One of Kerner's jobs was to authorize the opening of the chamber door after he determined that everyone had been asphyxiated by the Zyklon B. Although it was certain that all would be dead inside of eight minutes, he would look through the peek hole to make sure, as he liked to tell the others. They all knew he looked too long.

In the mysterious way that sometimes makes strange bedfellows, Penkalski and Kerner became friends. As the dentist grew weakened by imprisonment and by self-accusations of cowardice that he had informed Hoss about Cecylia, he needed to confide in someone who seemed strong and who hated the commandant as much as he did.

The hatred in Penkalski grew slowly at first, yet with Hoss's constant refusals to allow him to see Cecylia, he knew he had been used. He was reassured that she was well enough, even taken care of, but he could not see her. No reasons were given. Outside the games of chess, the commandant had become ice with him. Perhaps, he thought, because he had finalized his investigation into who might be stealing gold from the dead, and found no one. The conclusion forced Hoss to file a report to Berlin that there was no reason to believe the leak in the flow of gold was here in Auschwitz. Maybe it was that the dentist had taken an opportunity away from Hoss to deal with a culprit in his own way.

In the time between their dinner, which was slightly better than the meager portions for regular prisoners, the *Sonderkommandos* had some time to talk before lights out. The dentist found himself at first talking with the maniac about the day, the number of bodies into whose mouth he had dug, the amount of gold he had gathered, the farts of the dead. The topics were always so gross that they would invariably invite Kerner's interest. At least one person would listen to him, and not play verbal games. He was too stupid for that.

Eventually, Kryztof's loneliness began to talk. Never before in his life had he confided to another about his feelings. He even tried to joke about it at first, telling his companion that he did not know if his desperation was a full emptiness or an empty fullness. The maniac just stared. But he did not go away.

"Do you ever get lonely, Mietek?"

"What do you mean, lonely? How can lonely be here? I fool the Jews into believing they will get a shower. I have always wanted to be an actor, but I have never told anyone about that. They would not believe me. So now I am an actor, everyday, some days many times a day.

"Now and then, one of the Jews seems to be on to my act, and they get suspicious. I like when that happens. It is a time for me to see if I can really act.

"You know the little bag I have attached to my waist? It is my prop bag. I have in it a bar of soap and a washcloth. So, then I make a fuss to reassure the Jew that he will be taking a shower. I help him place his clothes in a special section of the dressing room. I even help him put a number on the pile, and tell him it will be right here when he finishes. I give him soap. Sometimes my washcloth, too.

"When he goes into the chamber with the others, I think I am a great actor. I have convinced him." He waited a moment before saying, "When I look into my tiny mirror, I see Mietek Kerner, the actor. And I make sure I get my props back from the chamber."

With a sort of envy, the dentist looked at him. He thought he was in the presence of a child in a man's large body. "I am glad that you do not feel loneliness," he said to Kerner. "I am beginning to have a case of it all day long. When I get up in the morning, it is not even me who wants to get up. I am ordered by someone else."

Perhaps there was a comedian in Penkalski, who persisted in trying to make the maniac laugh. "And when I do get up, the bacon and eggs are never done according to the way I like them."

He looked at Kerner's reaction, and he knew never to bring up the matter of breakfast again. Looking away from the maniac's scowl, he continued, "I am told that there are sometimes a hundred thousand people here in Auschwitz, and we know they die every day. Thousands. We help count them. I wonder where they come from, about their families, if they have children or friends. Or even someone they love.

"I wonder to myself that I can be around so many people, and still feel isolated. It is because, except for you, I have no one to talk with." He did not know why he said this. Perhaps it was a measure of his desperation to confide in such a man. Under normal circumstances, the dentist would never encounter a Kerner.

This expression of friendship by the dentist marked a shift in their relationship. Yet, he did not dare share the deeper sentiments of his loneliness, afraid an expression of them might be heard as a plea for an intimacy not wanted. He settled for the most intellectual communication, knowing that at least he would hear himself out loud while trying to disguise the depth.

He began to speak to the maniac about the "dearth of aromas in the camp," the "paucity of flowers," as well as the "destitution of camp conditions," when suddenly Kerner stopped him by merely putting up his hand.

"Stop whining."

Penkalski was jolted by the directness of the expression which seemed more sophisticated than he thought possible.

He asked Kerner what he meant.

"I am tired of the way you talk. You are always feeling sorry for yourself. Take what you can from the few weeks of your life that is left. Be happy. Here, take this half piece of bread I got today for some sewing string I found wrapped around the wrist of one of the Jews."

The dentist was so starved for this personal appreciation that eating the bread had the same effect as drinking a tumbler of whiskey. He felt almost giddy.

"Do you know that I cannot find if anyone is stealing gold from the dead?" he whispered.

Kerner whispered back, "No one is. If anyone was I would know, or it would be me."

The unknowing affirmation of his report to the commandant made the dentist's mind work in ways he recognized. Identify the problem, a pain in the gums, find the rotting tooth, repair it or pull it out. End of problem. His quest to find a thief had just been completed. By a maniac.

"What do you mean, the last few weeks of my life?" he asked Kerner who, by now, had the dominant hand in the conversation.

"You are a fool not to see around you. Don't you notice that in the time you have been here, many of the men you saw work at the furnaces are gone. You did not know that they have been cooked themselves?" His large belly shook in a synchronized amusement with the quirkiness of his own sense of humor.

"I figured. But I did not know."

"You are stupid for a smart man. Hoss and his men clean house whenever they think we have seen too much. You hear the big guns in the distance at night. It is nearing the end. And when it does, you and I will be killed because we know what has happened.

"I have been here longer than anyone, only because they think I am stupid and they think that I am a man without pity. I am useful. They think they know everything, but they do not. They do not know that I once tried to help an old woman—I like old women—to get off the line that leads to death, and go to the other one. She wanted to stay with her daughter and grandson, so she would not let me help."

He stopped talking, and looked down as if he were in some kind of deep thought. The loneliness in Penkalski wanted to ask him what he was thinking, but he dared not. He had heard the stories, and was afraid to ask. Yet he was glad to detect the small shadow of a muse who might have once lived in Kerner when he was a child. Something, maybe the residual gift of goodness, needed to express itself, and it simply popped out of his mouth. "I have done something terrible, Mietek."

Mietek smiled, as if any particular deed could be called terrible. Life itself was terrible.

"I have informed on a girl I knew in Oswiecim. I did it for good reasons. To get her away from a competitor for her affections. Commandant Hoss told me he would protect her in Birkenau and that I could see her once in a while. He was a liar. I have not seen her since she came here."

Kerner looked at him as if he was the madman. "How many times must you be told that you are a fool? That he is a liar. You are so stupid."

He did not say this in a crushing way. Rather, like an affection from a friend, an understanding between the two.

"I do not know what to do," Penkalski said. "I must make it up to her. She knows nothing about what I have done."

"What is her name?"

"Her name is Cecylia. Cecylia Brydinski. I do not hear the sound of her name much anymore."

The dentist's eyes glazed over. Kerner, took an almost sensual delight in the dentist's confusion, and began to fondle the ring finger of his right hand before saying, "Do you remember I told you to enjoy your last weeks?"

"I do."

"I have a way for you to enjoy your last times. It is a way for you to tell Brydinski you are sorry."

31.

Doing his best to cover his fear, the illustrator tried to effect a swaggering tone when he said, "I am Tyszka Dunajski. Here is a letter from Commandant Hoss that allows me to go about Birkenau and talk to anyone I want. It says that I must be accompanied by a German officer."

The soldier at the guard gate read the letter before cranking his telephone to make the necessary call. In a few minutes a well-polished SS officer joined him. It was clear that he had been instructed about his role.

"I will accompany you to where you would like to go," he said in a robotic tone. "Where do you want to go first?"

He wanted to see Cecylia, but he did not think it was a wise thing to do immediately.

"Take me to some of the guards. I speak only Polish."

"They are called the Death's Head units. They have been recruited by the SS from many different countries. I will introduce you to one who is from Poland."

The officer immediately took Tyszka to one of the young guards, pants and jacket neatly pressed, each metal piece of his uniform buffed, each a nugget shimmering in the light. He was holding a lengthy and supple whip with a leather shaft behind his back, one hand at each end. Legs spread, he was the picture of power waiting to unleash itself.

The SS man explained, "This man has authorization to talk with you about Commandant Hoss. He is working with Hoss. He will explain."

"I am an illustrator," Tyszka said. "I am sketching the commandant for historic purposes. Perhaps you understand that to get a person accurately, especially the face, it is necessary to know him."

The officer looked at him as if in a daze. Clearly, he did not understand. Tyszka sensed as much and shifted the inquiry.

"I can see the great things that Commandant Hoss does," and as a quick afterthought, "and you, the men who guard the camp. I want to know what the men think about the commandant."

"What do you mean, think about him? I do not think about him, and I do not think the men think about him," he said as he turned to the warden for support. Tyszka noticed the tiny, knowing smirk, intended to convey masculinity, playing about the guard's mouth. The self-conscious grin accented a large red blotch on his cheek

"I see," Tyszka said. "I know what you mean. What I mean is do the men like him, does he treat you well?" The questions were meaningless to Tyszka. They only served to buy him time.

"Yes, of course, he treats us like officers. We have a house, plenty of food, good wine, women when we want, the *frauen* block at Auschwitz. Most of them are Polish women, you know."

To keep the conversation going, the illustrator answered him, "No, I did not know."

"The only part I do not like is when the trains come in with the thousands of Jews. Sometimes some of them are dead already, and the cars smell like dead animals. I hate that smell."

Tyszka was immediately emboldened by the courage that comes from hatred. "Why are you here? I mean, why have you become a Death's Head's guard? Do you know what I mean?"

"I am not sure."

"I mean do you hate Jews and that is why you are here?"

"What do you mean, do I hate Jews? Of course I hate Jews. Don't we all?" he said, again looking at his fellow officer.

"I do not hate Jews," Tyszka replied without thinking. Knowing the risk, he was shocked that the guard did not take issue with his retort.

Neither was used to such conversation, and the exchange was becoming like the dance of a snake and mongoose maneuvering.

"Before this I was rotting in Katowice with this little police force in the city. No wages. Nothing. I saw the chance to have this job, and here I am. No, I do not have bad experiences with Jews. But this is a good job, and I do what I am told. Besides, I do not personally kill Jews. I simply keep order and guard them so no one escapes. If they try to escape, my job is to get them back and turn them over to Hoss's SS. But, again, I do not personally kill Jews."

Just then an older woman passed by, carrying a latrine bucket in each hand. She was on her way to dump them into one of the nearby pits when the Polish officer stopped her by putting his whip to her chest.

"Why are you going so slowly?" he asked her.

"I do what I can," she said in a voice so low she could hardly be heard.

He dipped the end of the whip into one of the pails before rubbing it across her cheek. "Move," he said. And she moved.

If Tyszka could have smashed him across his cheek, he would have. He wanted to ask him if he had a grandmother, and if she was that lady would he have humiliated her with urine. He knew, though, that questions like that could be answered better by the stones in the hardscrabble beneath his feet.

Instead, he looked at the man, and asked if they could move on.

Dressed in ordinary clothing, Tyszka looked out of place among the pinstriped prisoners. Some even looked at him, an unusual occurrence, looking at another in the camp without being asked. It was almost always considered intrusive.

He asked the officer if he could just stroll between the small wooden stables on the long pathways where horses used to run free.

When Tyszka was first aware as a young teenager of his ability to see into others' souls, he was often besieged by sadness. So much so that he wanted this sensitivity to leave him. He prayed that it would go away, especially when he could tell that a shadow was just lurking beneath the surface. This always scared him, as he no longer could tell what to expect. The math teacher, pretending to be understanding, would look at him, and Tyszka could know immediately the man's anger with students who did not reflect his precise expectations.

Even his art teacher in eighth grade, Mr. Wandelt, who let his hand run over a girl's shoulder down the middle of her back to the curves in her hips, could not hide his shadow from him.

The teacher had held as a coveted prize all year long that the best student in his class would have the privilege of sketching him, with all his classmates sitting alongside the artist to observe his technique. When the pervert couldn't anymore stand the students' laughter as Tyzska sketched, he got up and looked at the illustrator's pad.

There he was, a thin face with sunken cheeks and dazed eyes staring up as if in a simultaneous search for his soul and the pleasures of his body. It was clear from the full lips dripping saliva what Tyszka thought of him.

With a disingenuous air, he reminded the budding illustrator that he must always be careful when depicting things the way they were not. The irony was not lost on his student.

As he walked along the rows of the prison quarters, Tyszka began to feel a strange dizziness, one he had never felt before. He was woozy, yet he was certain that he would not faint. As long as he, too, was walking, most who walked past him did not look up. Each of their bodies was as tired and irritable as their mood.

It was nearing the time for the workers to return from the Farben factory, and perhaps he might get a glance of Cecylia, though he soon remembered the note from Hoss, and realized the authority it gave to him. He could simply ask to see her.

"I want to see a woman named Cecylia Brydinski who goes to work in the factory. When does she return?" he asked the officer-guide.

"The factory workers usually return about four-thirty. But you cannot see her then. She must first be counted with the others, and then have her food. It will be dark by then, and it is not good to be walking around here at night. You could be shot."

Just then the workers from Farben were entering the main gate of Birkenau. Several of them had fallen by the wayside, and their comrades were bringing them back into the camp in wheelbarrows.

In one of them he could see a young body that was partly covered by the lifeless body of another woman. The young woman had brunette hair tied in a bun. Tyszka's felt the shock of fear, and his heart skipped. If this was Cecylia, his anguish about Hoss and the compromise would be over forever, as he would have nothing left for which he wanted to live.

32.

The days at Auschwitz were speeding up. The number of Jews Hoss prescribed for the daily death quotas could not be met. Nor could the furnaces keep up. The pits were more frequently used now to kill and to eradicate evidence.

Prisoners were being forced to march more quickly to their work places so production would be increased. Night bombings at sites close to the camp were increasing in frequency.

Even clocks and watches seemed to be moving quicker. Time was being sliced into minutes that were thin. Signs that the war was coming to an end doubled the persistent dread of annihilation because now there was hope for life. As personal desperation began to subside, the stakes seemed to grow.

Although the soldiers under his command might find it implausible, the commandant, a creator of death, also bore in his body a sense of apprehension. But for him it was not that he might be killed, but that he might not be able to kill enough.

It was only recently that he had asked the dentist to play chess with him as a means of relief from the constant demands to meet the numbers. Besides, he enjoyed their verbal games, and expected no less from matching wits at chess.

If he beat the commandant, Kryztof thought, he might have much to lose, and if he lost, he might have much to gain. He concluded that playing chess with Hoss would become more than a simple game. In these delicate times, winning or losing might be for Hoss the tiny, but critical, element that could imbalance the daily equation of death at the camp.

Because Hoss bragged so much about the extraordinary number of Jews he was killing every day, and how he must be winning favor with the Fuhrer, it was evident that he would try to outdo his own record of 20,000 killings in one day. If Kryztof could just upset the commandant's routine for a day or two, maybe, just maybe, a few Jews might be saved from the increased pressure to kill as many as possible.

But if he was wrong about calculating Hoss's ways, if he won one game too many, he might set loose a personal vengeance that could easily add him to that day's list of dead Jews.

He thought it ironic that time was on his side. It was Hoss's to control, yet it was Penkalski's to squander. If he could prolong the games, maybe he could distract the commandant from his usual lust for killing.

Hoss did not know that the dentist was as competent at chess as he was efficient at running the camp. Penkalski had played chess since childhood. The experience did not make him a master, yet it did afford him some mastery. He knew how to control tempo.

"Commandant Hoss, I will play, but I do not wish for us to be timed. I think that the moves we make must be the result of our own skills, that they must not be dictated by a clock." And then, in an appeal to his ego, he said, "If you are as efficient at chess as you are at running Auschwitz, there will be no problem."

Hoss reveled in the cleverness.

"You flatter me again. Yes, we will play without time separating each of us from our brilliance. Let us begin."

It was clear to Kryztof that Hoss was no match for him. His moves were unimaginative, without flair. It was not so clear, however, if he should win or let Hoss win. He decided that, sooner or later, he must himself win or else his plan would be obvious. If he did win today, he must be certain to do it in a stumbling, almost accidental, way that would, at least, not trap Hoss's ego.

"I am, perhaps, the greatest of the camp leaders. Do you think so?"

The game began.

"I do not know how to answer. I do not know the others, or how many there are." He was always on edge talking with Hoss, and thought that his response might be taken as an insult. Perhaps Hoss was thinking if one were in the presence of greatness, what could it matter who else there was?

"About a dozen in the east, with hundreds of smaller ones attached, a few in Germany. So, there is your answer. Now what do you think?"

"I think I must take your word for it."

"For what? That there are other camps, or that I am the best?"

The dentist busied himself with setting up the pieces for the game while Hoss continued setting up Penkalski.

"You know how we Germans are trying desperately to rid the world of Jews. I have told you how we have other camps to do this work. No one does the work better and more effectively than I do. Under my command, the Reich has gotten rid of millions of Jews. When the war is over, the world will know the greatness of the deed. I am first among those who have helped. It is clear. The numbers say it is so."

The abyss of emptiness came over the commandant. "You can not see the greatness," Hoss said staring at Penkalski. "You are a Jew. You only know deceit and deception, power and greed. Hitler is right about you. And I am the answer. You do not know it, but *I* am the accountant."

In one fine, controlled motion, he swept his right arm across the chess board. Pieces flew across the room.

The dentist jumped at the abruptness of the move. His own edginess surprised him, as Hoss's tantrums were to be expected. Kryztof was beginning to see how common the man was, and began to wonder how someone with not much else beyond efficiency and hatred could have come to oversee the killing machine that was Auschwitz. Perhaps it was, he thought, his ordinariness that disguised evil and led him here.

"Pick them up. Let us now begin. First, I am going to have a whiskey, though there will be none for you," he said, as if the dentist was a child.

It took four hours before Hoss made a move so final in its stupidity that Penkalski could not ignore it. In a game of risks, a king could not be left open without consequences.

"Checkmate." he whispered, almost afraid to say the word that reduces an opponent to his wit's end.

The way Hoss had played the game was confusing. When he invited the dentist to play, he seemed to be serious and skilled. Yet, as time went by it was apparent that he was insecure about his abilities and easily rattled when playing on a level field. Although Kryztof's endless strategic moves with his pawns were intended simply to buy time, they threw Hoss off his mark, as if the strategy was designed to set him up for a move he had never before experienced.

33.

Kryztof had been hiding the diamond, his precious diamond, since the second day at Auschwitz. He was surprised when he found it, but not surprised to find it drilled into the teeth of the woman whose matted gray hair was still held together by barrettes in the high-style of the affluent.

He had sewn the diamond into the lining of his jacket, just below his armpit where he could press the inside of his arm on it whenever he wanted to make sure it was still there. In the camp black market where potatoes were traded for a sliver of soap, it was invaluable. Perhaps he would save it for Cecylia.

"Penkalski, I have told you that there is a way you can get the Brydinski girl to love you again." Kerner could always see the goodness of others. Yet, he saw the softness that often went along with it as a sign of weakness.

"Of course. I am interested. Please tell me."

They were sitting on the floor in one of the side spaces of their quarters. Although the wooden beds of the *Sonderkommandos* had thin mattresses, there was no privacy in the shared bunks.

"I am connected to other prisoners here and to the women at Birkenau," Kerner said. "It is not hard for me to get things done when I want. There is talk about a civilian walking around there asking people questions about Hoss.

He has also been asking about this Cecylia. I want to know if this is the man who fights you for her affections. His name is Tyszka. I have asked."

"He is the man," responded Kryztof.

"There are two ways I have to tell you how you can get her back. I can have this man killed. It is easy. An officer is bribed to find him violating a camp rule. He can be beaten or shot. It is simple."

The dentist knew that his answer would measure the level of decency left in him. "What is the other way?" he asked.

"You know that we are all going to die," replied Kerner. "Especially us Jews who work in the crematorium. It will be soon. I do not know about hating Nazis because they kill Jews. I am a Jew. What I do not like is their arrogant ways. How they order me about with their exact rules. 'Do this' now, 'do that' then. I do not see them laugh. Even the way they kill is withoutheart."

The dentist had not yet heard the man speak with this kind of fire.

"Have you ever seen a farmer kill a chicken?" Kerner asked without waiting for an answer. "If you tell anyone what I am going to tell you now, I will snap your neck the way a farmer snaps a chicken's neck. You hear a pop and it is over."

"I will tell no one."

"There is a plot. We are going to kill Germans, and while we are at it we will blow up the crematoriums."

Mietek waited, knowing that the dentist would need time to absorb what he had just told him.

"What do you mean, kill Germans? That is preposterous."

"What does this preposterous mean?" Kerner said.

Penkalski got up from the floor to take a step back, as if he was trying to distance himself from this man and his words.

"You are crazy! How can we, without weapons, kill Germans? They are everywhere. They have rifles in their hands, and pistols strapped to their sides. We have nothing in our hands, and wrinkled skin hanging on our hips."

"Keep your voice down. We have a way. Before I say more, I must know if you want to join us. It will be your way to make it up to the girl. When she hears about you, she will have, how do you say, esteem for you. I will ask you one time. Do you want to join us? Whichever way you answer, remember a chicken's neck is easy to twist."

To make his point, he picked up a small piece of wood lying in the dirt. He held it in both hands, pretending to twist it before cracking it over his knee.

"It sounds like suicide to me," the dentist responded. "I think I am better off staying here to be freed."

With a sigh, the maniac said, "Penkalski, every time I think there is hope for your brains, they turn to shit. You will never be freed. You are already dead. So, why not take that from them and kill yourself?" As he often did, he answered his own question, this time in a tight whisper that was almost a hiss, at the same time balling his right hand into a fist. "Be a man. Show the girl who you are. That we know things, that we shit on Germans."

The hair-trigger mechanism that set off Kerner's anger sprung. "You are a coward who pulls gold from dead teeth. You have started a new thing, a new specialty. You should advertise yourself, The Dentist Who Digs For—"

"No more!" Penkalski hissed back. "Do you think I like what I am forced to do? I hate what I do. I am not a coward."

Kerner knew it would be to their advantage to have the dentist with them. He saw how he was able to do his work, get along with others, even the guards.

"Look, there is a chance with the plan that some of us will be able to escape. You will have everything to gain. Now give me your answer."

After a lifetime of calculating, reinforced later by the diligences of dental school, spontaneity seemed reckless to the dentist. He surprised himself as he uttered, *"Yes."* It was as if someone else were saying the words. He hardly knew this man. He began to get lost in the thought that this could be a trap, a way for Kerner to bring favor from the guards, to buy another week or two by informing them about Kryztof's part in a non-existent plot. They would shoot first, later ask the questions.

"Good. Here is the plan." Kerner's voice snapped him back to the dirty floor where they were sitting. "If anyone comes near us now while we are speaking, we will talk about today's dead bodies. And how they resemble dead chickens." Just as suddenly, he said, "Stay here. I will be right back."

He came back with a piece of thin bread. Folding it in half, he said, "There are many who are involved. We have been preparing for a long time. Prisoners here and at Birkenau are involved. There is a farm on the outskirts of Birkenau where some of our men are sent to help the women plow the fields. These women will give us what we need." He stopped to rip the bread in half, and stuffed the pieces into the sides of his mouth before tonguing them onto his teeth for a quick chew.

"This is where you fit in. You must convince Hoss you have a suspicion that someone at Birkenau is stealing the gold. You have already convinced him that there is no thief here. Ask to be assigned there for a few days to snoop around. You will be our contact with the women. Tell him you need me for protection, now that things are getting wild."

He abruptly stopped to say, "Are you listening?"

"I have been trained to listen," Penkalski replied.

"Good. There are work parties of the women that go every day to the Farben factory in Monowitz. They walk, about forty minutes. The factory makes fake rubber. For this, they have materials that we can use. There are men here at Auschwitz who have worked in the mines and know how to make explosives."

"How can the work parties get the materials?"

"We have been bribing the guards at Farben. Mostly with things like cigarette lighters or tiny wedding rings the women have hidden in their bodies. Sometimes the rings have small pieces of diamonds."

Kerner was becoming agitated, even excited, as he spoke about the plan. Thoughts about killing could do that to him. Penkalski had to remind him to speak more quietly.

"We have almost everything we need, except one ingredient for the grenades we plan to make. We have nothing left to bribe the guards."

He stood up to confront the dentist. He started nose to his nose, then slid the tip of his own nose along the side of Penkalski's, and across the grime on his cheek before stopping at his ear to whisper, "I want you to steal gold for us."

The recent change from counting the odds before placing his bets to placing his bets before knowing the odds was almost sufficient for the dentist. However, the urgencies of this day demanded more. The gears of his brain must never plod again. A transformation was needed.

He thought about the diamond that he had sewn inside his jacket. Next to the hope that he would see Cecylia again, it was his most valuable possession. It was a risk, yet maybe he could use the one to find the other. Perhaps, just perhaps, when she found out that he had given it to help kill Nazis, she would learn to love him. "I have a diamond. Bigger than you think could fit in a tooth," he blurted out.

As if disbelieving what he had just heard, Kerner replied, "You have a diamond?"

"Chances are I will have no need for it. You can use it for the materials we need." On an impulse, he quickly added, "Do not hug me!"

No bear hug, no words of thanks. Just a quizzical look from the maniac, as if his feelings had been hurt. Penkalski wondered how it could happen that a monster's feelings could be hurt.

"We will use it for the explosives we need. Give it to me."

"How do I know that what you are telling me is so?"

"You don't. Now, give it to me."

The dentist twisted his body to the left so it would be more in the shadows. He put his right hand inside the middle of his jacket, then ripped the stitches so he could touch the diamond with his index finger. He slowly fingered it up the wall of the small pocket he had sewn into the jacket. Despite repeated efforts, he could not keep the diamond from falling back down, again and again.

It was only when he began to use his middle finger that he had the proper touch to successfully pull it up the cloth. He rolled the piece of beautiful hard carbon between the thumb and middle finger of his right hand, wondering where it would go next, hoping it would not decorate the hand of a German.

He squeezed it between his two fingers so that it hurt. If he could no longer have it, he would at least have an impression of it.

34.

Three o'clock in the afternoon, the time young Tyszka always liked best in the early springtime. He tried to imagine the blinds of night falling on Oswiecim in mid-May. The sun beginning to disappear before its final burst into amber spray. Peepers filling the night, like little zitherists, with lyrical overtures to tomorrow. He could smell cookies in the oven. And was that the sound of his mother's voice calling him home?

But, it was not springtime. It was December in Auschwitz and Tyszka was about to meet the poet. By now, the guards were aware that he was armed with a letter from the commandant, and they were used to seeing him chat with other guards, as well as with some of the prisoners.

The poet had a reputation in the camp, and it was a contradiction of nature to discover that his assignment was at the horrible place where cruel biological experiments were done on women. Tyszka showed the letter at Barrack 10, and asked to see Abraham. The guard showed him to a small room, bare except for two chairs, and ordered him to close the door and wait.

In a few minutes, there was a delicate knock at the door. Tyszka opened it and saw a tall and thin young man who was called the Bard of Auschwitz by the more literate among the prisoners.

"I am Abraham Cykiert. I see you are not a prisoner. But I know who you are, and I am happy to meet you, Tyszka Dunajski. Shlomo gave me your letter about Cecylia last week. I read it a hundred times before destroying it. I was going to throw it into the latrine. But then it was so beautiful I decided to eat it, so maybe it goes only a different way."

They both laughed.

"It is good to laugh, Tyszka. It has been a while for me.

"I hope you know that I am only eighteen years old. So that is not a lot of experience, not a lot of loving. In fact, no loving at all. I will tell you that I have never been in bed with a woman."

Resisting another laugh, the illustrator said, "Neither have I."

"It matters little, Tyszka. We will have our day. I can tell from your letter how much you love this woman. I know why we stand speaking freely for a few minutes. I know, too, from your letter, that you are an illustrator."

"Abraham, I am grateful to you for writing a poem. I only wish that I had more than two potatoes to give to you for your work."

"It is enough. My father had one and I the other."

"Please let me see the poem. I am excited to read it."

"I have it in my right hand, on a folded piece of paper I stole from this place where I work. It is a terrible place. I do not want to talk about it. When I shake your hand, I will place the poem in your palm," an unconscious deference to watchfulness.

As he said this, he hunched his shoulders down and clasped his hands on his lap. Tyszka thought he was going to cry.

"It is the best I can do," Abraham said. "Sometimes, though, it is given to the young to know much. I have been here for a year and a half. The death I see tries to suffocate me. But, I will not allow it. The Germans say that words are the means for Jews to tell lies."

Tears welled up in his young eyes.

"No, my new friend," he stammered, "Words give me joy, they save my life. When I was a child, the school teachers called me a *dyzio,* you know, annoying. Because I was always writing poems, or sitting in a corner reading books when I was to be doing something else. Mathematics, oh, no, not mathematics. Not again."

He was talking his age. After so long, someone was listening. He was a teenager again, instead of being the Bard of Auschwitz, the touchy young man who wrote when he was supposed to be sleeping.

Acting his age did not last long.

"Do you know German, Tyszka?"

"A few words, not worth much. Why do you ask?"

"I know some I learned at a course I took one summer in Poznan. I fight with some of the words at night and during the day when I want to close my eyes. Do you know, Tyszka, the hardest part is the aloneness of being here. I used to live in a world I thought was civilized. I was being prepared to be in the world. But, here I am, abandoned should I say?"

"Yes, abandoned is a good word for it."

"These things are closing in. I recognized when this began. And then I vowed to myself to not let them crush me, even when I can feel them squeezing my heart."

He stopped, as if these thoughts really were at that moment squeezing his heart.

"About the body, I cannot suffer more or less than my circumstances say I will. But, I fight the death of my mind by thinking about my poetry. That is how I stay sane. So I think. But, lately I am obsessed by words I learned that summer. I try to find the answer to what they say to me. I find myself drifting toward the answer, and I do not like it. If it is the answer I think, I will go insane. For a poet, that would be redundant."

As Abraham looked at him with a small smile and eyes cast again to the ground, Tyszka could tell that he was embarrassed. The poet was so young that his face had not yet grown into his large ears. Tyszka wanted to touch his shoulder, but did not dare, even though they were alone. Fear of breaking some rule seemed to have infected him.

"Friend," he said, "what are these words you fight?"

Leben und tod—he started to say the words in the German he had learned in Poznan that summer not long ago.

"It is of no use if you do not understand the words I hear," he said to the illustrator.

"But, I do know some German words. *Leben und tod*, life and death. They are the fundamental words."

"That is the point," Abraham responded. "I once thought I knew what it was, you know, the difference between the two. Life was going to school, being with friends, my mother, my father. The future. Now, the life I lead is . . . I see death here, and in the piles everywhere. In the gas chambers. The smoke. There is no more life. There is only the flame."

If I could only bleed for him, Tyszka thought.

"It does not make sense any more. I try and I try to make sense of it. What is the test, what is the lesson? A test, a lesson, I think. Is life a school? No, I think not."

Tyszka was listening, and the poet could not stop talking.

"But, where is this God of our fathers? He should be here, here in Auschwitz, destroying the evil doers. He should be scooping them up with big hands and throwing them into the ovens, throwing them in before they are dead."

Ever the poet, Abraham remained close to what he could see and touch and feel. Tyszka knew the tight knit that could exist between a man and his art, and he knew that when the knit got too tight that the mind of the artist might disappear into the mist. And so, he began to be afraid for Abraham.

"I do not think really that God has hands. I do think that God has a body. He is not a man or a woman. But, if he is God, he is powerful, and if he is just, he would be vaporizing them, not us. It does not make sense to me, so I continue to think about *leben und tod*."

"I do not know what to tell you, Abraham."

It was as if the poet did not hear him. So he continued to speak the thoughts he pondered when he tried to go to sleep at night, or when he tried to close his eyes.

In a voice growing increasingly thin, the poet said, "I say to God that if he is not good and loving to everyone, then I do not want any part of him. I would rather go to the pits. This life is like a test without answers."

The illustrator had never before heard anyone speak this way, at least among the Catholics in Oswiecim. He thought it courageous of Cykiert to show his fist to God.

Abraham suddenly stopped, as if he were coming out of the mist, and looked at Tyszka.

"I am sorry. I am going to shake your hand now and give you the poem. It has been my privilege. To be with you today also. Sometimes, I want to go to a mountain and scream hard so that I will burn out my throat and not be capable of speaking anymore. But there is not even a pillow to cover my lips. I look up and see the smoke and know that there is no way I can stop myself from thinking *leben und tod*. It is my nightmare."

They shook hands so tightly that Tyszka was afraid he heard the poem being crushed. It was, in fact, the sound of a white-coated doctor's jackboots crushing the scrabble beneath his feet. He was walking with a group of little children to the gas chamber while holding their hands and giving them candy. The always present and much used loudspeakers were playing a Polish children's song called, "Mommy, Buy Me a Pony."

35.

For three days Tyszka had tried to meet with Cecylia. The guardian SS officer said that was impossible. She was busy before work, and again after the walk back from Monowitz, until bed time, he said.

When asked, even Hoss opposed his wishes. "I do not want to get between two lovers of the one girl. It is not good business."

"But, Herr Commandant, I have been getting wonderful information about you from those under your command, as well as others."

Hoss interrupted, as if he had been slighted. "They are *all* under my command here, everyone here."

"That is clear to me. When I speak to the guards, officers, *kapos*, the *Sonderkommandos*, they say the same thing. All except the one officer who was not complimentary."

Hoss's rampant egotism was hard to read. Some days it was needy, like a plant unwatered. If this was one of those days, the remark would draw notice. .

The remark was being parsed. It was one of those days.

"What is it that this officer says about me? Who is this officer? Auschwitz or Birkenau?" He was angry that anyone would dare.

Hooking a super egotist with a two-part bait was risky. Getting him to chase the lure was easier than enticing him to bite the hook.

For some time now, the illustrator was aware that he was barely holding on to the truth of his art. And now he was beginning to drink a poison most subtle in its effects. He was about to maneuver another for personal benefit.

"What I can tell you, Commandant, as it is said, with all due respect, is that in a moment of weakness, I am sure, he said of you, "*Hoss nieder, frieden wieder*"—Down with Hoss, up with freedom. He quickly added, "You know that I do not understand the German language, yet these words are easy to know, so poetic. I have found out what they mean. Not a compliment, though he seemed tired and irritable that day."

Tyszka had noticed before that when anger was brewing in Hoss, his left eyelid drooped and quivered so that it appeared to become a butterfly's wing flapping.

Now the risk. "I will tell you his name after you have let me see Cecylia. Only then." *Lieben und tod,* he thought.

Already stuffed with power, the commandant liked sometimes to play with relinquishing power. It was a crafty way to be sadistic by taking the worm off the hook and allowing its prey to wander about freely for a time. On another day, he might have shot Tyszka on the spot for his arrogance. Realizing this, the illustrator could feel himself trembling as Hoss paused before responding.

"I do not know why, but you are lucky that I find you amusing. Go see your Cecylia. But, remember, I have told you already about our last sitting before I will go to Berlin. It must show my patriotism to the Fatherland and my loyalty to the Fuhrer. As well as my vision. That I am the man most important in making good things happen for Germany. Others up the line might have given the directive to kill Jews, but mine was the last order to make certain it happened."

Worn down by weeks of maneuvering, Tyszka felt almost giddy with relief. "Yes, Herr Commandant, I will be certain," he replied.

Early the next morning, a truck picked up a bewildered Cecylia from Birkenau and drove her to Block 29, the *frauenblock*, at Auschwitz.

"Where am I ?" she asked, getting out. The driver looked her over with an exaggerated slowness, halting systematically to stare as if taking off her clothes with his lustful eyes.

"You will see." Taking her by the arm, he rang the bell. A stout German woman in a cream-colored evening dress opened the door. She seemed to be expecting the visit.

"I have been ordered to deliver the woman to this block," the driver said. He then locked his left hand on Ceclia's right elbow, and gave her to the madam before turning abruptly out the door.

Cecylia could not see Tyszka sitting in a small room off the middle of the corridor, as if waiting for a turn. She was confused and began to make a commotion with the big woman who was trying to tell her where she was, and that she was expected by a man called Tyszka who was waiting inside. Finally, Tyszka heard his name repeated ever more loudly until the childhood playmates realized at the same time what was happening. He opened the door and there she was.

She first stared at him to check her sense of the real, then opened her arms to his embrace. For some, a joy like this locks time inside the moment, deprives it of its compulsion to move on. For Cecylia, the realization that she was actually *with* the one whose unique mystery she was discovering transcended the moment, now a symphony of emotional notes so complicated that they were difficult for her to understand.

Tyszka could feel her taut and thin body shivering, and he wanted as hard as starlight to protect it from harm. He imagined himself drawing a special kind of cocoon for her, one that could resist fire until hell moved away from Poland. Or at least away from here.

Tyszka always thought that the scales which measured their worth had favored her. Perhaps now they were finally balancing. Whether because he was free to come and go at the moment, or because their paths, side by side for so long, had been mixed together by the swirling iniquities around them, he did not know.

He looked into her eyes, now so tired. "Cecylia, you are crying." Her lips were closer to his than ever before, and he could feel the warmth. "I don't have a handkerchief," he said, trying to offset the awkwardness he was feeling by being practical.

He bent the index finger of his right hand into a kind of scoop, and slowly ran it up, then down, both sides of her wet cheeks to spread the drops back into the smoothness of her skin. The care and gentleness of the act contrasted with the violence Cecylia had been witnessing at Birkenau and she began to remember the days long ago when she was happy.

Is it possible for my heart to swell? she thought, *and could it burst?* "Please hold me again, Tyszka. Hold me tight."

Tyszka did as he was asked.

He also was in the fullness of his joy, and was not sure what to say when she backed away.

"Do you know where we are, Cecylia?" He could tell she did not. "We're at Auschwitz, and this is the brothel. It was the only place that has privacy this early in the morning. I am sorry. Come with me," he beckoned. "Here is a room for us," pointing to the small room where he had been waiting for her.

It was, of course, an awkward invitation. "Please, it's all right," he said, as several of the women, half-dressed and resting from the work of the previous evening, peeked from their rooms to see about the talking in the hall.

The room had a single bed with clean sheets, a fluffy pillow, and a small table with a candle. A tiny picture of an angel hung on one wall.

"Here, please, sit on the bed, and I will sit against the wall. We have some time. I don't know how much."

Tyszka's heart, from childhood paced more by anxiety than by the the rhythms of love, needed time to express itself. No matter. Cecilia was too smart not to know that there might be little time left to them.

She bent over from the bed to touch his face. Tyszka pressed her hand against his cheek, and could feel perspiration in her palm which was warm, small, and soft. He rubbed the palm into his cheek so that tonight in his bed he could touch the spot with his own hand before cupping it to his heart. If the way she was leaning over had not been so clumsy, he might have kept the position forever.

"Why am I here with you, Tyszka? What is happening? Where is Kryztof?"

"So many questions, Cecylia. You are here with me because I have become a liar. You are here because the authorities found out that you helped me and Kryztof deliver food under the fence to the prisoners." The struggle to reveal the dentist's role in her imprisonment was nagging at him.

"I wanted to see you. I have something for you. The only way to meet you was to create a lie to the commandant about someone. I am not happy about this. I try always to be a good man, to do what is right. It is right for me to see you." The impulse to express the way he felt about her was expanding inside him.

"Cecylia, how I love you," he found himself saying in a voice that no longer shook in the way it had before when he tried to say this thing. Today was different. Somewhere along the way, the declaration, in moving from his brain to his heart, had become powerful. He did not even think about how she might respond.

"How are you?" he asked. "Your hair—are you OK? I have worried about you. I have become a stranger to myself. I want to live. I want you to live. I sketch falsely. I do not know who I am." He could not stop himself, a virtual machine gun splattering personal concerns.

Cecylia knelt by his side. "Shhh," she whispered, before kissing him on the lips.

"Tyszka, I think of you all the time. I think of you when I go to bed at night. I think of you when I wake up. And when I work at the factory, I think only of you. There is nothing more that I want than to be with you." With a shy trust in herself, she added, "For the rest of my life."

She kissed him again, long and hard, before giving him a hug half diminished by their awkward positions.

Getting up, she sat on the bed again. A little distance was needed before she could express her second thoughts.

36.

"Tyszka, please listen carefully." He got up from the floor, and sat close to her on the bed. She did not move away from him, as she feared what she was about to say might offend him.

"Everything is happening fast. One day I was at home, the next I'm here. I know I have broken the law by helping prisoners." She looked resolute before saying, "But the punishment is insane. I do not have the words to tell you of my sadness, my anger. If I could only pin my disappointment in the Germans to something I have experienced before, I would deliver my thoughts to that place to understand what is happening to us.

"I am afraid, though—" She stopped before taking Tyszka's hand and saying, "Isn't it funny that our little village has given us so many good things that I am now tangled in confusion by what I see? When I try to make sense out of it, I cannot. It is as if my thoughts go so far and then they are paralyzed."

The illustrator was relieved that, in spite of his recent accommodation to his fear, his instincts seemed intact. He could tell that Cecylia was still steadfast and strong, no matter the numbness of her brain.

Before he was able to respond, she put her hand on his mouth. He was content to bathe in the gesture, and he would remember it later when his lips would tingle at the thought.

"I think I am in love with you," she said. "But I wonder if the feeling is real, or is it another thing I cannot understand now, because of what is happening to me, to us? If suddenly I was no longer a prisoner, and Kryztof was no longer a prisoner, and we were returned to Oswiecim, would you and I be lovers?" She paused thoughtfully before adding, "Or just friends?"

The words deflated Tyszka, as if the fire of his love for her was being extinguished by the sprinkle of her uncertainty, especially when she said, "I am not even sure where Kryztof is. Do you know?"

Tyszka knew right then that he might place some certitude on her feelings by letting her know what the dentist had done. Again, he played with the idea for a moment.

"I only know that he is here, a *Sonderkommando* dentist, and he is treated well. I have asked the commandant," he responded in a voice so thin that she could hardly hear him.

He would not tell her about Hoss's personal interest in her, about why the *kapo* who gave out the evening soup always dipped the ladle deep into the pot for her, so that she would get a full serving of the vegetables that fell to the bottom.

Cecylia could see the confusion in Tyszka's eyes. Trying to take back the moment, she said, "I hope he is well. I will tell you that I only think of him as a friend, whenever it is that I think of him."

For a while, at least, Tyszka felt refreshed, that he had the upper hand on Kryztof.

"Cecylia, look what I have. It is a poem for you," he said while taking the wrinkled paper from his pocket. "I did not write it. I am not a poet. But I did write down my thoughts about you for a poet. His name is Abraham, and he is here in Auschwitz."

"Tyszka, that is sweet of you. Let me read it."

"No, please. Cecylia, I will read it to you. Then, in a little way, perhaps, it will sound like mine."

"Yes, of course. Please read it."

He held it in his left hand. The flimsy paper began to shake.

"I am so nervous," he said.

"So am I. No one has ever before written a poem for me."

"I will begin," he pronounced. "It is called 'A Wish'. Here it is:

Life emerged and I think of you.
There is the clay creating matter
to a form most perfect, and you.
I want to be breath of your breath,
flesh of your flesh, light of your light
in the knitting of time when
we will emerge from this inferno,
holding hands forever.

"Please read it again, Tyszka. Slowly," she asked.

He did, and she said, "Thank you, my sweet heart." She then put the poem inside her blouse. "I will hold the poem next to my breast so I can feel the paper when I breathe," she said, self-consciously.

"Stay here," he ordered. "I will be right back."

Several minutes later, he was back with a little dirt in his pants pocket. He put a small twig from a dead tree on the table. He then pulled out several berries and a piece of sketch paper from his back pocket before unfolding its quarto size into a full sheet.

"I am not a poet, Cecylia. I am an illustrator, and I am going to sketch you right now. Please sit on the bed here," he asked, patting the spot. He then moved the table near her. Two times he worked up as much saliva as he could in his dry mouth before spitting it on the table so that it formed a small glob.

He took several pinches of the dirt from his pocket and dropped them onto the saliva before squeezing the berries into the clump for color. He asked her to spit into the mess before stirring it with the twig which would also serve in place of a brush.

"I will do thin strokes, Cecylia, so it will dry quickly. You must hide it from them."

Spit and dirt combined did not have the naturally smooth and porous quality of charcoal, and prevented his strokes from sliding gracefully. Tiny grains of sand made bumpy lines yet, under the circumstances, they would do.

"Do not be concerned if I seem to stare at you some-times," he said, suddenly beginning to feel the possibility of failure. Perhaps his recent false sketches of the commandant had left him without the purity of his art. He might have robbed himself, thrown away the gift.

If I can only find her with the twig I will be happy, he thought. *I will know that I have not lost my capacity to translate the truth to paper.*

The task at hand was made doubly difficult because he had not yet tried to work with tools like these which he had recently heard about in the camp.

He decided to depict her face in a profile two-thirds her real size. It was the best way for simple strokes, an approach he must take because this new way, he could tell, would not allow for texture.

The eyes. Especially when they sparkled with the light of her love and enthusiasm. Always the eyes first. There was love, of course, yet the vitality he had always admired in her face was almost gone. He told himself that it was there, invariably there as one of the signs of her grace, but now hiding, a little girl behind the window curtains, at least for a while.

It was easy for him to find the eager child. He simply took her by the hand, in his imagination, and led her to the window where a twist of his wrist mated twig to vision.

If there were a genetic blueprint that guides the morphing of flesh in the formation of beauty, Cecylia's face, the illustrator had always thought, followed its code exactly.

Yet today, altered by his experiences of the past few months, and stunned by her haggard appearance, he realized, slowly, that she did not match the perfect design inspired by the romantic conceptualization he had of her.

The symmetry in her face, he began to notice, was imprecise. Perhaps the lobes of her ears were a trifle long. And maybe the jut of her chin was too assertive, yet barely perceptible. Her upper lip seemed too thin to match the lower.

His strokes were lean and simple. There was no room for error, no eraser. In truth, he did not want one. He would know in a few minutes if his ability to depict the essence of a subject's soul remained intact, and by the unfolding of the work, he would know if the essential quality of who he was had changed.

As he worked, he felt that clouds were lifting and the sun was revealing itself. He was with his beloved. And at the same time, he was the illustrator practicing his craft with materials that somehow, in their primitiveness, allowed him to express the completion of his artistry.

Not even when he depicted the innocence of newly baptized babies did he work with such a confident flourish as on this day when what he created was different. Was it possible that he once knew the truth of his subjects, and now he knew it *more* fully? Could that be?

Tyszka felt weird. His illustration of Cecylia was complete. As he picked up the sketch paper from the little table, he stepped back, holding it with both hands slightly outstretched. For just a fraction he felt what it must be like to be God who could see the Cecylia that He had in mind. Today, now, in this moment, Tyszka could see on paper what *he* had in his own imagination seen of her. And it, too, was good.

Looking, he knew that his art and his soul were more tightly bound than ever before. The thin lines of the illustration, marked with spit and clay, revealed Cecylia as she was. Each part looked at by itself, as Tyszka was accustomed to doing, was not perfect. Their symmetry was even slightly flawed.

Yet, she was altogether more beautiful than any woman he had ever seen. If an epiphany of the spirit could sometimes show up as a sacred presence, Tyszka knew that at that moment he was full of the grace of awareness. He was bewitched, as never before, by Cecylia, by the elegance of her soul, the mystery of her uniqueness.

Within the dreariness of the circumstances, he was doubly dancing in his heart. He was in love, and the illustration, in its peculiar simplicity, wed the truth of his vision with the reality of her spirit.

"Here. It is done," he said, handing the picture to her.

As he looked at Cecylia, he became troubled, haunted again by the question that never let go, *Where are you, God? Why have you created the wonder I see before me, and then abandoned her?*

He pondered, too, his own fate, and how that would affect her, whose presence gave him the chance to regain himself. He was afraid that finding himself today was going to be his undoing tomorrow when the commandant was ready for the final illustration.

Cecylia broke his reverie, saying, "Thank you, Tyszka. You have made me radiant in the picture. And do you know that it makes me look happy?"

She paused before saying, "I am happy. Especially when I am with you."

37.

The men in the barracks housing the *Sonderkommandos* met every night after lights out for three consecutive nights. It was risky to break the rule against the lights. If they were caught, it would be the end of them and of the plot to blow up the crematorium.

Each barrack elected a leader who coordinated the planning work, which was led by Mietek Kerner. The system was simple, though vulnerable. Each of the four leaders, numbered one through four, coordinated the plan by seeking out the three others the next day. They did this in the time between rising in the morning and roll call, usually a chaotic time without supervision by lazy guards who were tending to their own morning rituals. The brief meetings were efficient, yet susceptible to the counter-bribe of a corrupt guard.

Kryztof's diamond became the indispensable piece needed to complete the bracelet of bribes at the Farben factory to acquire the explosives necessary to make a few hand grenades. Under the best circumstances, the guards would have been guilty of extortion for the little they delivered in return for the diamond. Under the present circumstances, Kerner was satisfied that he got what was needed.

A critical discussion among the elected leaders in the meetings was whether to complete plans for the revolt or to wait out the liberation that was coming fast from the east.

Kerner prevailed by brute force, as well as by the vigor of his logic. Ovens and pits could no longer get rid of the evidence, and the bodies were beginning to pile up, he reasoned.

"We are the last ones to handle the dead," he told them. "We have seen the treatment. Cut the hair. Rob the gold. We are the last to know. And the first to die when the end begins." The men could tell that he was becoming tense, a dangerous presence. In the end, though, it was the vacant stare of the psychopath that won them over.

"I will make arrangements with the guards at the farm today to bring back the last of the stuff we need." It was also a chance for him to look at the women, unkempt and earthy, in the fields.

"I want another man with me. Who will go?"

Immediately, Kryztof volunteered. "No, your job at Birkenau is done," Kerner snapped at him. "Because of you, we are certain that the materials our workers have smuggled from Farben have gone to the women in the fields. They have been reliable. I have been told how you encourage them. If you try to go back there now, it will be suspicious. Always remember how they watch." The gnarled index finger he put into the dentist's face was a forewarning of consequences if he did not pay attention. "You will not go," he said, finality in his tone.

"Pass the word," he continued, "If anyone shoots his mouth off, I will find him myself and I will rip his tongue from the mouth with my hand, and he will choke in his blood. The meeting is over until tomorrow. Malgorzata, you will go with me."

Kryztof lingered. "Mietek, I must ask you to do something for me today. When you go to the fields."

"What is it ?" he responded curtly, as if bothered by the request.

"Each of the times I went to Birkenau, I have tried to locate Cecylia. I have not been able. I have been cautious not to stand out, to be only a seeker of the thief who steals gold, and I have passed the messages. I want to give her a note. Here it is," he said, holding it out to him.

"How can I do that? I am busy with other things. You, too, tell me to do this today, to do that tomorrow."

"You will find a way."

Reluctantly, Kerner took the note.

If they looked far, the prisoners working in the fields around Birkenau could see forever-rich plains and beautiful rolling hills. Most of them, though, did not want to look, did not want to feel the weight of pain that came from imagining who or what could be out there. For many, staying alive in a place governed with casual indifference to death was enough to bear. Hiding under a shroud of personal apathy might, at least, afford some protection against the sting of suffering.

Bibiana, a onetime robust Pole, was the leader of the women's group that worked the farm at Birkenau, and received the materials taken from Farben.

Her group was small. A tiny safety pin fastened on their blouses near the left collar bone identified them to the men who came to coordinate the work. As many as possible would do their work near her, almost skeletal now as compared to the last time Kerner had seen her.

"The powder is in the small sacks there," she told him, pointing to a pile of dirt. "Each sack has strings attached. Bend down to tie your shoes. Strap a bag, top and bottom, to each ankle. Take two apiece. The guard has been won over, so you do not have to worry at this end."

Guided by an impulse of gratitude that lingered in a brain cell perhaps not yet killed by the excesses of an unbridled past, he said, "Thank you." And then, "Take this," handing her half of a potato he had saved from the night before.

"When will it happen?" she asked.

"I do not know," he lied, knowing that it was to be tomorrow. "When you hear the explosion, you will know.

"Before we go, I am looking for a woman named Cecylia who came here from the village several weeks ago. I have something for her. Not from me, but a friend called Kryztof, a dentist who takes teeth from the dead. I think it is a letter."

"Yana," as she was called, seemed more interested in looking at Malgorzarta who, in the golden years, she could tell, would have been worthy of her love.

Kerner suddenly sprayed the field in a gush of words he presumed to be humorous. "The girl is young, long brown hair, a playful walk, very white teeth, good bumps in the chest."

Yana did not laugh, but simply looked at him as if to convey that he was acting like a fool. He did not like this. He did not like a condescending look from a woman.

He wanted to confront her, but he knew from his years on the streets to be careful not to disconnect himself from what he needed.

But, as always, he needed someone to blame for the anger bubbling within him.

In the way that it often happened to him without warning, he was compelled to point his finger at someone. Like the answer to a sick prayer, Kryztof came to mind.

"This dentist is in love. With the girl Cecylia. He is a crazy man. Do you know that he identified her to the commandant for helping other Jews? He thinks it was a way for him to see her, and to keep her away from another man who lives in Oswiecim.

"And now he asks me to give her a letter, as if she would want to hear from a man like that. I must be going. I do not have time for taking care of lovers."

He was agitated, but it felt good to release a little steam.

"Take this. Give it to her. Or throw it away. I do not care."

"I will give it to Anna over there. She has just been assigned to us from the barber shop where she did not cut the hair close enough. She is Cecylia's friend."

They quickly strapped on the bags of powder and slowly walked the half-mile back to their barrack, never deviating from the path guarded by the Death's Head units of the SS.

Kerner's thoughts were of the bloodlust that he would satisfy tomorrow, Malgorzata's about his wife and children, and how a woman had looked at him with warmth in her eyes.

38.

Next to the loneliness of going to her wooden bunk at bed-time, the worst part of the day for Cecylia was the two hours between arriving back at the barrack from the factory at Monowitz and eating the slim supper of soup, designed by the camp nutritionist to cause inmates to slowly consume the stores of their own energy.

Hoss was once heard to remark, in a feeble attempt at humoring camp administrators who were concerned about overcrowding, "Do not worry. In time they will eat themselves."

At the machine shop, Cecylia could imagine potatoes coming from the lathe. Once she thought she saw borscht in the cylinders. It was blood dripping from the tip of her pinky finger sliced by a cutting tool.

The guard told her that she was fortunate to be skilled at the machine and took her to be stitched at the infirmary, where she did not linger. Early on, she had been warned never to stay there where an impulsive doctor, drunk on the wine of sadism, might inject her with a lethal needle.

After standing in the freezing cold for the completion of roll call, the time spent waiting for soup was routine, though critical. Stitching socks was important for survival, and cleaning mud from boots mandatory. Today, though, would be different for Cecylia.

Anna was waiting for her in their barrack.

"I have news for you," she said in an overly eager way. "It is a letter from a man. Yana gave it to me for you. An important *Sonderkommando* from the camp sent it." She added, "as I understand it," so as not to inflate her roll as a messenger.

Yet, a transaction such as this in the camp was so unusual in its romantic implications that Anna could not help herself from writing a few lines into the drama.

"Yana said that the man who wrote the note is the one who turned you in. To see you, she said. Like it's a hotel or something here."

Maybe it was only the need. Or the boredom of days without spice. No matter, it was too late when Anna saw that the look on Cecylia's face laid bare the implication of her words.

"Cecylia, I am so sorry for what I have just said." She covered her mouth with both hands, as if this would prevent her from ever speaking again. Just then, the unexpected occurred. Anna's well of tears, long dried up, yielded one small drop that trickled down her cheek.

"I want to die," she said, as she reached to Cecylia.

"It is all right. You have always been kind to me. You meant no harm." She yanked the sleeve covering her right arm over her thumb and used it to dry Anna's tear.

"Look at me," she said. "It's all right," and she waited to make sure that it was. "You can give me the letter now. It's all right."

It had always been clear to Cecylia from the circumstances of her arrest that someone had informed on her. It was equally clear that only two people knew about how she helped with the vegetables that night. As sure as she was that it was not her beloved Tyszka, she was certain now from what Anna had blurted out that it was Kryztof.

The letter was smudged, and as she opened it a few specks of dirt from the farm fell out.

My Dear Cecilia,
I have missed looking at you. When I heard you were in Birkenau, I tried to see you, but it could not be done. Sometimes, I think I will never see you again. I will not have the chance to explain to you that I have tried to be a good man. But, it has not always been so.

I think I have harmed you by only thinking of myself. I hope to explain this. Please know that I am sorry, and I am trying to make it up to you. If we were in Oswiecim, I would ask you to marry me. Yet I can only say now in our prison: I declare Cecylia Brydinski to be my lawful wedded wife.

Written in loving words, it was signed the same way.

Cecylia, though, did not care anymore. She was exhausted by caring, and she was beginning to feel the numbness of an escalating hopelessness. If it was not for the recent visit with Tyszka, she might have already sunk into despair.

She found that the note with its proposal meant little to her. She did not trust the dentist anymore. Glad of this, she read the expression of his confusion one last time.

Then, while she waited for the soup, she tore the letter into tiny strips, from top to bottom, then each strip crossways into the smallest parts possible until they looked like grains of rice in her hand. If she had salt, she might have chewed the tiny pieces into mush before spitting them out.

She would go to sleep that night thinking about Tyszka, yet a little baffled that she would not be dancing in the dreams that come to lovers.

And while she was sleeping, the plotters at Auschwitz were working furiously through the night to construct three small and powerful explosive devices that would be pivotal in the uprising which was now set for ten o'clock the next morning.

Sneaky little Fryderyk was the cruel and slick kapo who ran the black market at Auschwitz. The network was a thin string of coordinated prisoners and guards who could get you whatever you wanted, provided you had food, goods or, lately, outside collateral. With the sounds of war coming closer each day, those who had a remnant of hope knew how important it would be to establish links in the outside world that would be sources of food and shelter, even transportation to destinations, old and new.

The wheel of his dealing extended to the farthest reaches of the camp. He knew everyone's comings and goings. It was natural for the *Sonderkommandos* to turn to him for help in arranging the last planning and work session that was needed to coordinate the revolt.

His job was to bribe guards to look the other way, except for the barrack responsible to make the home-made grenades. For a few cigarette lighters and two bottles of schnapps, they were expected to disappear for the night.

The word was out. Each of the men was to be at his appointed position at ten. Immediately after the explosion at the furnaces, two grenades would be thrown into the units housing the Waffen-SS officers. Everything was going as planned until Kramer noticed that some of the officers who were usually inside the targeted quarters were outside. It was already nine-thirty when he asked Fryderyk about two long lines of children walking side by side, holding hands, boys in one line, girls in the other.

"I have heard they are the children of Negro soldiers brought here from Africa by the French after the last war. Of course, they have married German women. I have also been told that Hitler thinks the Jews brought them to the Rhineland to infect Germany. They will be sterilized this morning."

Kerner began to get agitated. He noticed that many of the guards who supervised the crematorium were escorting the children, keeping control with candy bars. He was upset because these guards would be out of their quarters when the explosions went off.

He quickly thought about calling off the uprising for another day. Yet, he knew that the momentum of planning under difficult and delicate circumstances had reached the point of no return. There simply was no time to break it off without being exposed. Besides, he knew that all of the *Sonderkommandos* would soon be dead men, especially now that the Russians were coming, because they knew too much.

The uprising had been difficult to coordinate. So few watches, no central clock. He knew immediately that a change in plans would result in certain and immediate disaster.

He was especially upset that Otto Moll, the SS major and head supervisor at the crematorium, was leading the children's parade. Moll was strong and cruel, and Kerner hated him. It would be a disappointment if the marble of this muscled man was not shattered by one of the grenades.

Kerner walked as fast as he could, without attracting attention, to the place he had assigned to himself. He must first go to the housing unit where the axes were hidden, strap one under his pants, and wrap a blanket around a grenade with a fuse, then get to one of the basement elevators used to bring bodies up to the furnaces.

As soon as he and another *Sonderkommando* carried one of the gassed in a canvas litter to the elevator, he unstrapped the ax, and held it in his hand under the stretcher. When the door opened, Kerner let loose a savagery that matched the worst of brutalities inflicted at the camp.

He took two steps out of the elevator, let go of the body and, with his right arm, made a tight and powerful arc that cut the neck of one guard through to his windpipe. The other guard, paralyzed by the swiftness of the execution, accepted his fate without protest.

Kerner quickly lit the fuse of the grenade before placing it on one of the mobile tables that was used to slide dead Jews into the same furnace that he had recently observed receiving a still-breathing child.

Fifteen seconds were enough to return to the basement before the explosion that signaled the beginning of the revolt rocked the crematorium.

The officers' quarters, usually occupied at this time, were practically empty. One SS was killed while shining his boots, another seriously wounded by the remaining grenades.

By now, hand-to-hand fighting began in the mud and gravel pathways lining the crematorium building. It took about forty minutes for the pistols, rifles, and machine guns of the SS to overwhelm the stones, hammers, and axes of the prisoners.

After being shot in the shoulder by a tower sharpshooter, Kerner was held down by *kapos,* hoping to ingratiate themselves, before his face was caved in by the rifle butts of two of the Waffen-SS.

Most of the others were killed. A few escaped, only to be recaptured within the hour. Investigations were held over the next few days. With the exception of Kryztof, whose name was tortured from a lonely Malgorzata yearning for his children, the instigators from both camps were hanged with wire at various places around the camps. For three days, their purple bodies twisted in the cold, as a silent warning to the restless. And as a symbol, Hoss fancied, of power retained.

39.

Kryztof made sure that he was needed at Birkenau on the day of the uprising. He convinced the committee of the insurrectionists that the confusion created at the crematorium would spread to Birkenau. He told them that the Waffen-SS controlling the camp would throw down their weapons and run from the imminent arrival of the Russians whose memories of atrocities committed on their soil by the Einsatzgruppen units of the Waffen ran hot.

He would organize a women's escape, he told them. Quietly, he had gathered information from the women about escape routes, fences that were not electrified, and the places where guards were few or could be bought.

His attempts were mild enough not to attract too much attention among the women, yet they had enough verbal flourish to convince the committee of his intentions.

The chaos did not reach to Birkenau. As soon as the news of the revolt came from Hoss's office in Auschwitz, Kryztof was arrested as he ran carelessly toward the west end of the camp. He thought that was the least guarded place, and the best way to freedom.

"I thought you were smarter. You could have completed your sentence. You could have gone back to your little village. Ah, yes, the respected dentist once again."

Hoss moved slowly from behind his desk, walked pensively across the room before opening the office door to direct his secretary to bring him a cup of hot tea "with a little something in it."

"I do not suppose you will tell me if you found a gold thief in Birkenau?" he asked.

"No, Herr Commandant. There is no thief there. The camp is clean. Your report to Berlin is accurate," he answered. He was still trying to find a way to get on the good side of Hoss.

"Good."

For a minute, Hoss chose the tension of silence before pretentiously asking, "I don't suppose that any good will come of another game of chess, do you? You are always clever, and you would allow me to win."

With these words, Kryztof knew the instant draining of all hope. He knew that his motives had probably always been transparent to Hoss, that he himself had been used in some perverse way. That he was mostly a diversion, a playful challenge to the commandant who had been playing a game of real-life chess with him. If he was to delay the end of the game, he must be imaginative.

Hoss stopped tinkering the moment, and said, "It is hopeless for you now." He walked toward the corner of the large desk where he kept his Luger. Strapping the holster around his waist, he pointed to the door.

"Let us go for a walk. It is a nice day today, especially after yesterday." Two Death's Head guards accompanied them to the open courtyard.

What Hoss was about to say was relevant only to his growing need to humiliate.

"What about the girl? Your girl? We have no proof so far, but we think she is involved with yesterday. She is one of the girls that go to Monowitz each day. We know almost everything, so do not play stupid with me."

"I do not understand what you mean," the dentist said, actually trying to play stupid so obviously that it might work.

Slipping into the formal way that often accompanied his sadism, the commandant said, "I will tell you, Dr. Penkalski, we will make a deal. A simple one. Turn her in or you will die, now, today, on this spot. Tell me the truth."

The challenge was abrupt, startling. There was little time to think. Even in the anxiety of the moment, though, Penkalski remembered that he had already betrayed Cecylia once, and how that had preyed on him. Perhaps he could redeem himself today? But how? And could he trust Hoss? Perhaps no matter which way he answered, he might become another victim of the commandant who was growing increasingly ruthless and needy in his desire to kill Jews as the end drew near.

It was possible, Krystof thought, that Cecylia was dead, and the commandant was playing a sadistic game with him, one final humiliation. If she was dead and he turned her in, no harm would be done, and he might survive, if only because Hoss always seemed to have some respect for him. Yet, if she was alive and he betrayed her, she would surely die.

Most of the things in life that had challenged the dentist's courage had come in small doses. Standing by his father day by day over time, saying *no* to an invitation that might ignite a craving, or saying *yes* to the denial of a shameful need that might get him through the night.

Nothing, though, had made him ready for this moment when he knew in the marrow of his bones the immediacy of the truth that yesterday's sins could be expiated when the offer of redemption presented itself. Yet, he was standing terrified in muddy pebbles between a man seduced by hatred and two trained murderers. A choice with life-threatening consequences must be made.

"Commandant Hoss," Krystof said, "do you remember when I was first brought to the camp, how you told me that you would arrange for me to see Cecylia?" He hoped the reminder of a promise not kept would touch the vestige of a high-minded instinct Hoss might once have had.

Hoss could not hide a faint smile of admiration for the dentist, always trying, always playing for the upper hand, even when he no longer had any cards left. He seemed amused at the nervousness in Krystof's voice, the sweat on his brow.

"You know that I have not yet seen her. I have reminded you, an honorable member of the Third Reich. But, you have been too busy to arrange it. Perhaps now, before the end comes to her, or to me, you will allow me to visit?" Hoss looked away, as the dentist continued his plea in an almost begging way.

"It is a man-to-man request," Krystof said. "You know how it is," he continued, more like a question than a statement.

With fatigue in his voice, the commandant said, "I am tired of your games. Very tired." And then he whispered, "So, I ask you one final time, was she involved in yesterday's murder of my men?"

Even Kryztof knew that he had finally played every card. At times like this, he had always resorted to his most basic instinct to avoid consequences with grave penalties.

In a tone as low as the whispered question, he answered, "Yes, she is one of us."

"Are you sure?

"Yes," he said again.

Hoss's inevitable fulfillment through brutality had always been understood by Penkalski. Perhaps the dentist realized this when he lunged at Hoss as the commandant unholstered his pistol. At the same time the guards grabbed his arms.

Whatever it was that he whispered into his ear made Penkalski's eyes grow wide, as if he wanted to see forever. Hoss put the pistol against the dentist's chest before unthrobbing his heart. His body was left to lie in the courtyard of the camp.

40.

Except for the dread, the feeling of waiting was much the same as he had experienced on occasion as a little boy. Lungs wrapped in a net of tingles. Brain and heart, tuning forks vibrating childhood fears about dark places in the cellar.

Tyszka's wait for the summons from Hoss was heightened by Russian artillery, as well as by the explosions coming from the crematoriums for the past two days. Trying to wipe blood from their hands, and wash ashes from their mouths, the Germans were blowing up the furnaces.

Nervousness was plain to see. The guards began to run to and from their duties, as if quick movements in the dust might cover up their tracks.

The fading polish from the boots of the SS was matched by uniforms worn more casually each day. Collars were loose, insignias missing. The officers were divesting themselves of bric-a-brac medals, and Iron Crosses that marked congratulations for the slaughter.

As hard as he tried to find out about Cecilia, Tyszka could not get a definite answer. A few thought she had already been sent toward Germany with thousands of other prisoners as part of the continuing work force needed by the Nazis. Another said she had seen her in Birkenau the day before.

Exhausted, he waited for the knock on his door, which came late in the night. When he had first arrived at the main gate of Auschwitz, he knew the irony of the message above the iron gate, "Work Shall Make you Free." Tonight's work might make him free. He knew, though, if he kept faith with his gift this evening, he probably would die.

The commandant was sitting behind the big desk, a touch of scotch in his belly.

"Before we go any further, my illustrative friend," he muttered. Then he stopped to say, "Do you get the joke of the words?" as if he were about to keep a manly covenant with Tyszka.

"Yes, commandant, I get the joke," he answered through the melancholy of his smile.

"Before we go any further, tell me the name of the one who criticized me."

What a strange moral confrontation for the illustrator. He wanted to respond, "It is Lt. Kramer," yet he knew that if he told such a lie, he would slip another rung down on the ladder, lowering the starting place for tonight's climb.

Instead, he resorted to the truth that Hoss needed him today, his last chance to have a perfect portrayal of the face that school children would look at in history books a thousand years from now.

"Please, commandant, if I tell you now, the anger you will know might appear in your eyes. That is, if you would like to show up in the books as an angry man. If that is how you would like to be known, I will tell you now."

"We will wait. Now, get on with the business."

As soon as his charcoal pencil reached for the paper, Tyszka sealed his own fate. It was as if the need to depict the truth was inscribed in the biology of his body.

What struck him first was what was not in Hoss's face. Flat eyes without the glimmer that carries hope. Lips that kissed his children, perhaps without the warming catalyst that transforms routine to love. A left cheek not full, and slowly sinking into the hollow of his deficiency while slightly pulling his lips to one side, making his face appear a little contorted. Even his nostrils did not seem to be open wide enough to breathe. He was a man, Tyszka thought, who looked a bit starved for air.

As always, he began with the egg-shaped head. It is not possible, at least not generally so, for a person's eyes to grow closer together in a short period of time. Yet, that is what happened to Hoss. It was as if he needed to pinch them into a focal point different from the usual. Tyszka first outlined them as he saw them. Only then did he realize that eyes so close to each other could not possibly meet at a normal point of convergence. They would each cross through the usual end point, before going off into the distance. Hoss appeared to be seeing through people and into an anticipated future, with little ability to see where he was.

Though it was easy for Tyszka to execute this anomaly on paper, it was difficult for him to make the choice to portray it as it was. The long nose with tightly pinched nostrils anchored eyeballs that almost touched. It was not a depiction that would please Hoss.

Would he dare now to form the fleshy sacks under eyes halfway down his head? To the artist, they seemed like bags of tears never used. *No matter,* he thought. *It is what it is, and I will show it so.*

"Commandant, would you like me to shade in your evening beard?"

"If you think it makes me appear more handsome, put it in."

All he could see was the straggled shades of an uneven growth. But he put it in.

The chin that used to point did so no more. It was as if the great bone of the chin had lost its way.

As always when he was centered in the truth, Tyszka began to work quickly, as if excited by a strange drug. This was the way to joy for him, and he was now in it, precisely in it, swimming in it.

He tried to suppress the hallelujah that began to trip across his lips. But he could not.

"What is that song you hum?" Hoss asked. Before Tyszka could answer, he was reminded that he must finish quickly. "I am going to Berlin in the morning. The Russians will be here in two days. My staff has its instructions. No Jew will be left alive. Hurry."

The revelation of Hoss's intentions quickly brought the illustrator's thoughts back to Cecylia. He could lose faith with himself today and perhaps, by doing that, ask Hoss to spare her. A false stroke here, another there, and it would be done. He would tell Cecylia later and, if she loved him, she would forgive his compromise.

The commandant's disclosure had abruptly wrenched Tyszka from the source of his joy. The dogs of his internal war were beginning to yap at his heels again. Ironically, after knowing of Hoss's plans to kill every Jew in the camp, Tyszka did not want to see the malignant heart of the man revealed in his face. Though ordinary, it was not an appealing face. Perhaps it was a bit distorted in the configuration of the parts, he began to think. But, it was not an evil face. Tyszka was finding it difficult to see the truth. He was beginning to wonder if the gift was gone.

"Commandant, I am almost finished. I have always noticed your eyes." And then he asked a most curious question. "How do you see your eyes? What I mean is how do you think they look to someone who sees them?"

The questions, convoluted as they were, confused Hoss, though he seemed flattered to be asked.

"They are eyes with a vision. You know that it is the way I want them to look."

He continued. "They are eyes like the Fuhrer's. They see what must be done." Then, courted by the illustrator's interest in him, he fell into an embrace of self-revelations.

"Do you know how this all got started, Dunajski?" he asked eagerly.

"I do not know what you mean."

"The camps, here, killing the Jews."

"No Commandant Hoss, I do not," he answered, for the first time calling him by name.

"Our men rigged up the exhaust from a truck to kill hundreds, maybe thousands," he said proudly, "of Russian prisoners. In farmhouses. At the same time, even before the Jews were sent here, I was concerned about getting rid of the rats and mice we had, especially at Birkenau in the stables. I began to experiment with the Zyklon-B gas to kill them.

"Fortunately, at the beginning when we were getting started, Himmler came around to the camp to see how we did. He is a genius, you know. He simply put together the poison gas I used for the rats and mice with the farmhouse technique, and ordered us to build a gas chamber. The furnaces came later when we realized that bodies were piling up.

"Here is the good part," he continued. Tyszka seemed held by a spell of disbelief at what he was hearing.

"Himmler took this information to Hitler. I know this from someone who was there, a friend of mine in the SS. Himmler told the Fuhrer that if he, the Fuhrer, wanted, he could kill Jews this way quickly.

"They decided to do an experiment here in Auschwitz. Under my direct supervision, we killed two thousand Jews in one day." For emphasis, he repeated, "In *one* day."

By now, Hoss was falling into the weave of his own story.

"It was easy for us. The Polish people were willing to turn over Jews. Himmler asked the Fuhrer for permission to gas more. It was the way, he said, to get rid of every Jew in Europe, the way to unite the Fatherland. It did not take long, I am told, for the Fuhrer to nod his head. This is how it began."

Young Tyzska did not know what to say, though the artist in him was responding. It did not make a difference to him to ask the question, as he probably would be dead soon.

"Why did Hitler say yes?"

"I do not know. I can guess. I have always thought of myself as someone who understands him, his way of thinking. I have been near him, once. But, I know many people who have been near him, even close to him in the work. I am happy to say that he is like me. You might say I am like him. Yes, that is better."

"How do you mean?" Tyszka asked.

"He is practical. He knows how to get things done. He hates Jews. He thinks they are liars and cheats, communists. He once told someone who told my friend that he cannot stand the smell of Jews. He does not like the smell. I think I do not like the smell." He began to smile.

"Hitler does not care. People do not exist for him. I mean really they do not exist. He lives by the will. Whoever gets in the way of his will must be destroyed. Even the children he charms. They too would suffer if they were in the way. I think when Himmler explained to him that there was a method to get rid of Jews quickly and efficiently, he seized the chance. He does not have the slobbering mentality of the weak. It is missing in him. That is his strength. Jews are numbers to be reduced, to be eradicated. I provide the means."

His arms began to flail so wildly with pride that Tyzska thought he might be having a seizure. Yet, he continued to rant.

"I think he is like me. Of course, he, and not me, gave the order. But, when I was asked—and I was not at first directed to do this—to gas Jews, it gave me satisfaction. That is all I know, that it gave me satisfaction. I did not care about their lives, or about their deaths. I kill them like I step on a cockroach. And it does not bother me. Yes, the Fuhrer is like me. He does not care. He cannot care. He only hates."

Tyszka realized that he could take no more of this. He knew that he could not compromise himself. He knew that to save himself he must preserve his gift.

"Finish your business, and I will let you go," Hoss said suddenly. And just as quickly, he asked, "You are a Catholic? Am I right?"

"Yes, I am a Catholic."

Tyszka began to look at Hoss one more time. He would complete the sketch, leaving the eyes for last.

After listening to Hoss's rant, the face looked different. There was something hiding underneath the ordinariness of it. Perhaps it was the faces of the millions he sent to the chambers who were executed before their names were even recorded. Or maybe it was the innocence that was also his at birth.

Tyszka was confused. Hoss's common face appeared to be changing in front of him, so that it was like a hand-blown window pane, reflecting now this look, now that. It seemed to be a series of undulating imperfections appearing in the frames of a movie seen at a slow speed but progressively moving faster.

Always ready to have their way, Hoss's self-righteous efficiency and discipline were suddenly present in the smugness of his lips. So that when Tyszka looked at them, hard sounds about "fire" and "ovens" could be heard.

The shadows of Hoss's cheek and beard grew darker, his nose began to bend, and the once fleshy lip, always ready to express the excesses of his ego, grew as thin as the tip of Tyszka's charcoal pencil.

Just as suddenly, the illustrator again found himself in the joy of his gift. He would allow the instincts of his heart to complete the strokes that would form the face of Hoss.

Never before had such a lightness of hand guided his way. And never before had the strokes that completed the eyes of a subject precipitated a change of this magnitude.

The illustration was complete. Nothing fit. It was a discordant form, a grotesque monster, half human, half devil.

Tyszka had seen faces like this before. Though only in flashes that he did not always comprehend.

41.

"I am done, Commandant Hoss."

The reality of his own words, implacable and strong, struck him like a foreshadowing of the force he knew would be released as soon as he showed Hoss the illustration.

A momentary reprieve was offered as Hoss's aides ran in and out of the office to take files outside for burning.

"Tell me first who criticized me."

Clinging to the minute gained, Tyszka answered "Ask Lt. Kramer. He will know. It is not my place." The glazed look that signaled a coming storm began to form in Hoss's eyes.

Depending on the commandant's need to vent anger, Tyszka knew that he might be dead in the next minute, though he decided to face the minute without having to bear any more malice.

"Here is your picture," he said, sticking the paper in Hoss's face, just as he expected the commandant's pistol to be stuck in his.

He wondered if he would hear the noise of the gun exploding, if there would be the pain of a slipped razor biting, or if he would just fade slowly like a child without a melody to soothe him to sleep.

"Dunajski, you are almost as good as they say."

Tyszka moved quickly from the certainty of a death sentence to doubts created by the inner whispers of disbelief.

"I do not understand. What do you mean?"

Hoss was so preoccupied with his likeness that he did not hear the question.

"There is something odd about my eyes. I cannot tell what. Just odd."

Dumbfounded by now, the illustrator asked to see the drawing paper.

"Fix it," Hoss demanded with a determination equal to Tyszka's resolution not to fix it.

"Is it that there is not enough imagination in the eyes?" the illustrator asked the commandant.

"Yes, that is it. I cannot see the dream in the eyes. It is my work, my life, to kill Jews. I have nearly succeeded, yet I cannot see that in my eyes. Fix it!"

He had already sketched the darkness of the soul in Hoss's eyes, as well as the disordered nuances of a face infected by a black heart. Yet, with the immediacy of the order from the commandant, he had little time to reflect upon what was happening.

Tyszka felt himself being pulled by a strong force like the one that seized him when he was seven and fell down the muddy incline of one of the hills that surround Oswiecim.

Such was Tyszka's lust to live in the truth that the commandant's reaction to the drawing angered him. On the day when he slid down the hill, he tried to hold onto anything that might stop the fall. Today's first grasp at an explanation was that he had, in fact, lost the gift, that he could no longer see the truth about others.

Could it be that he only imagined he loved Cecylia? Could it be that the sound of her voice, which he loved to hear, struck a chord he had conceived to accommodate his own need to *be* loved?

He could not grab a hold of this thinking. Of course, he loved her. And, yes, he wanted to imagine her, for it was a way to realize the richness of his love. He could hear music in her voice, and receive its unique sound because he could. That was part of the simplicity of loving. It was merely a regaining of wholeness.

Yes, that was it! He understood. Hoss could not see the truth of who *he* was. He had covered the completeness received at his birth with so much brutality and cruelty, had accepted and repeated so many lies, committed so many murders, participated in so many deceits, that he could no longer tell who he was. His heart had become so crusted over by the dark canons of hatred that it was no longer available. He had, probably long ago, aborted his heart, and was ruled now by the principles of disrespect nurtured by an unattended intellect that had surged toward madness. It was as if, in squandering the divinity of his birth, he had changed his nature.

It was now apparent to Tyszka that the eyes Hoss wanted him to fix in the illustration were worse than odd. In repudiating the gifts of the heart, Hoss had developed a way of seeing that was without warmth, compassion, or ordinary considerations. It was a lens that refracted the light of truth so that he could no longer see himself as he was, but only as he wanted others to see him—a visionary hero of the Third Reich.

Tyszka looked at the finished portrait and then looked at the knotty mess of perversions sitting in front of him. He knew that his gift was intact, that he had today regained his own soul.

"Did you put the dream in my eyes? I do not have all day. I have told you that I must go."

Hoss was yelling at him, at the same time that Tyszka was yelling in his head at the God of his fathers, the one he had learned about in grammar school. Each time he compared the illustration to Hoss, he knew the abandonment of Cecylia, of everyone in Auschwitz.

Where are you, God? he thought. *I look at this man here, and I want to think only that he too is free, that in the freedom he has decided to murder Jews. They do not have a say. So you have made Hoss into a God who is free to kill. We are trapped in a world without goodness.*

Intensely in his own thoughts, Tyszka could barely hear Hoss shouting at him. Perhaps that was good because at the same time as the commandant was shouting, the illustrator was reprimanding God. It might have been unbearable to know at once the voices of two gods, one a cold-blooded killer, the other a not-speaking Word.

Suddenly, Hoss got up and went toward the pistol on his desk. The hard metal of the gun barrel sticking into his cheek brought Tyszka back to the room.

"Give me the picture," he shouted to the illustrator.

He examined it carefully, and said, "Better." And, although Tyszka had not yet re-touched the eyes, he replied, "Yes, better."

"Let us go outside now," he commanded. As soon as they reached muddy gravel, Hoss placed his pistol into Tyszka's stomach and whispered into his ear the words, "Have a nice day."

It was the first time Tyszka had seen the commandant laugh. As he placed the pistol back into its holster, he said, "We always play our games. Today, I win the game."

And then, "Leave now. Run away into the woods. It will be like hell here tomorrow."

Tyszka would never see Hoss again.

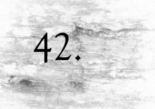

42.

By bribing sneaky Fryderyk with tobacco, Tyszka learned that Cecylia had already started her journey as one of the thousands of prisoners forced to march to the munitions factory at Czestochowa in a desperate effort by the German authorities to quicken a dying war effort.

The woolen shawl, given to her by a fellow prisoner who worked in the area where the personal belongings of Jews were sorted, made the difference on her journey. Like some of her fellow workers, the woman took from the dead whatever she could give to the living without getting caught.

After fifty miles of running and marching north in the cold and snow toward Czestochowa, Cecylia was chosen as part of a smaller group that was heading due west toward the electronics camp at Nordhausen in Germany. Fending off the sticks and stones of camp life had made her strong. She knew when to get to the back of a line, and when to get in front. She knew when to run and when to run faster. Energized by a relentless determination, she had taken the daily walk from Birkenau to Monowitz and back again as an opportunity to exercise a different set of muscles, and the enforced silences as a chance to think about her future.

The hunger of days and the coldness of nights killed many, yet the threat of being shot to death for trivial infractions held the group together. If they could find an empty barn or a pigsty along the road, it was permitted to sleep there. And if, by luck, a farmer opened his doors to their knock, it was acceptable to eat if food was offered.

Under no circumstances, though, were the prisoners permitted to rob from the earth. Both Himmler and Hoss considered their Fatherland and its yield sacred.

As the prisoners crossed the border into Germany, farmers guarded their barns and rejected the importunate knocking of Jews at their doors.

Cecylia would not let herself yield to the memory of a warm house with meat and potatoes on the table. She thought of the one piece of bread they received in the early afternoon each day as a promise of plenty rather than a call to resignation.

After the ninth day of forced marching, encouragement could no longer substitute for food. Cecylia enlisted the cover of a moonless night to go into a nearby field to look for potatoes waiting to be snatched. She took whatever she could fold into her shawl, then came back to share them with the others.

She slouched by the side of the road and began to rip hunks of potatoes with her teeth, now pitted with grit. No matter. The pleasure of sucking juice and cutting the hard pulp of potato with her teeth before swallowing gave her body an instant satisfaction. She was no longer eating herself.

Suddenly, though, she heard footfalls crunching the frozen snow. Looming in front of her was an SS guard, one of the last to stand fast while most of the rest fled.

"We have told you, Jew lady, that if you steal food on this trip you will be shot." And, as an afterthought that might later relieve his conscience, he asked, "Is this not so?"

Cecylia stood frozen in the snow, yet in the absolute clarity of the moment she comprehended that she was about to die for eating.

At the same time that he poised his pistol for the death shot, a figure, thin and white like a ghost, came out of the darkness.

"What are you doing?" she screamed.

"I am killing a Jew," he answered.

"You must not do that. The war is almost over. You can go home. We can all go home," she shouted.

As if a prophet, he said, "The war is never over."

"Besides," he said, "she has broken the law. She is a symptom of the Jew problem. She feeds her mouth with German food."

Giving him a stern lecture, the skeletal woman retorted, "You cannot shoot her now. For your own sake. The Russians are behind us, and the Americans are in front." Something was making sense to him, yet he did not know what.

Suddenly, he knew when she said, "They will know who you are." Pointing her finger at his face, she repeated, "They will know who *you* are. By the red blotch on your cheek. You cannot hide it, and it will go away only when you are dead."

The sounds of over-used and under-maintained truck engines, laboring to pull hefty loads of stolen goods toward Berlin, were heard leaving the camp. Other trucks, more official looking, carried the personal belongings and furniture from the curtained brick houses with picket fences that were built for Gestapo officers and their families on the edges of Oswiecim.

The need for sleep restrained its demands that night. The noises of mass movement were constant, and many of the guards were preparing to run away, discarding their uniforms. The remaining prisoners, hungry for the certainty of information, talked through the night.

Rumors were stoked by those who peeked outside. "They are leaving," some said.

"We are free," said others. The more perceptive, though, knowing that not every SS had left, tried to calm the palpable anticipation of morning's light.

When the noise woke Tyszka, he looked with his binoculars into the camp grounds. Nazi guards were running this way and that, while *kapos* were running that way and this. Meeting would have resulted in instant death for the kapos who knew names and rank. In his imaginative way, he thought of the activity as cockroaches scampering in the dark after someone has turned on the light.

The killing of over two million Jews at Auschwitz had been done in organized and systematic ways. *Kapos* had been trained to handle them smoothly and politely, asking them to place their shoes and clothing into neat piles and at specific spots in the preparation rooms so that, "after the shower," they could locate them easily.

This day, though, would see brutality so awful that its execution would haunt the camp long after its wood was taken to rebuild Polish homes, and the bones of its buried dead sifted again for gold.

Whatever order there might have been was now gone. Except for those deceived by duty to stay, most of the guards had fled the camp during the night, leaving the remaining inmates stunned, dazed, and disorganized.

In a frenzy to throw away the SS uniforms that marked them as murderers, some of the guards killed prisoners in order to steal the dirty rags from their bodies and merge into the anonymity of the camp.

The most recently imprisoned, still energetic, yet knowing the keen of hatred, were aware that the tide had turned, and began to organize in groups of three or four.

They first raided the kitchens for food and then, sensing the breath-taking fear that seized the remaining guards and some of the *kapos* about the abrupt reversal of their lives, selected, as if by instinct, the most vulnerable and began to beat them to death with shovels.

A few guards shot back yet they, too, quickly realized that begging for a mercy undeserved was all that was left. In almost every case, they begged the wrong gods.

Tyszka could see the Russians coming a mile away from the east, shouting while firing their guns in the general direction of the village. Afraid he might be hit by a bullet, he bent down on a knee, and stuck one eye of the binoculars out the side of his window.

Several hundred Russian soldiers, mostly men, were marching toward Auschwitz as though they were going to a party. Many behaved as if they had just come from one.

Soon, Tyszka could see them indiscriminately shooting Nazi guards, and in small groups groping female prisoners before pulling them into barracks. It was all beyond the grasp of his understanding. He thought that the lens of his binoculars must be converging on one of the lower rooms in hell.

43.

"My son," the bewildered Dawid Dunajski said, looking up from his little day bed, "what is happening?"

The tone and substance of the question reflected the inert quality of mind that had been his since he was gassed by Polish soldiers who took up the cause of Germany in 1918. The smoky green of chlorine gas had disturbed the fullness of his thinking and the flow of his words, but never the love and respect he felt for Tyszka's mother. Most of her friends told her that she lacked common sense to marry Dawid but, lucky for Tyszka, her sense was wise rather than common.

"Father, the war is ending. The Russians have come to our village. I do not know yet about their purposes, but you must stay in the house because they are shooting anyone who gets in their way. If they come here, give them what they want. I will be back as soon as I find Cecylia. I have what I need in the two satchels. And I have gathered vegetables and potatoes for you in the kitchen."

He repeated, "It is not safe for you to go outside now. Everything is crazy here. Do not worry about me. I will walk in the woods and in the fields, and I will come back to you as soon as I can."

It almost broke Tyszka's heart to look into his father's eyes. He did not know why, and did not think it silly, that he saw in those eyes the same dependent look he had seen in the eyes of his beloved cats when, as a child, he was becoming aware of others. In seeking to find Cecylia, he might lose his father.

"I have asked Mrs. Brydinski to look out for you. She has told me that she will come to see you every day. Be patient with her, my father, as she sometimes grows irritable. It does not have to do with you. It has become her way."

He bent over and kissed his father on the forehead. Neediness was in the old man's eyes. Tyszka kissed him again, and then pressed his cheek against the damp spot as if to seal his love. Cupping his father's hands into his own, he felt like he was falling, a parachutist trying to hold the weave of things before letting go.

He headed north toward Czestochowa.

The freezing cold nights of central Germany's January were as extreme as a death sentence. Unlike some of the others, Cecylia had felt only the tap of its chilling finger. Many were deadened by the cold blow of the wind. After several days and nights marching through Germany toward Nordhausen, it was becoming more and more clear to the SS guards that the Russians would soon over-run them and the long line of their prisoners. The remaining trucks that carried the once solid soldiers of the Wehrmacht, now broken and trying to get away, were running them off the roads. Bombings were more frequent and, with a prescience built on knowing the pulsing of the earth, farmers continued to close their doors to everyone.

The time had come for the last of the Fuhrer's loyal followers to carry out his wishes that no Jew was to remain alive.

The prisoners were ordered to line up in groups of one hundred.

"You are free to go wherever you want." As bewilderingly simple as that. There was not a sound from the prisoners. Freedom was, at least for them at the moment, a doubt, a thought, something that existed only in the mind.

Cecylia knew that real freedom for her was not only being released from the constant specter of sudden death. It was a release from a lump in the throat, and from the pain of emptiness. It was being willful again, going and coming wherever she wanted. Speaking her mind. Mostly, though, it was being with Tyszka.

The romantic love songs of Poland and the nostalgic lyrics of the Klezmer street bands began to play in her heart. Abraham's beautiful love poem, and the dreamy urges of hot-blooded desire for Tyska thrummed in her loins. Yet, a more primitive realization, no less real for its girlish conviction, was growing in her. That he sparked in her the desire to play, the willingness to dance, the joy of possibility. Quite simply, just by being true to who he was, he could return her to the promises arranged for her by the universe on the day she was born. If she could just see him again, they would stand together, and a benevolent sun would sweep its warmth over them.

The shaky-legged dream, now rising strong in the cold and snow of this night, just as suddenly collapsed when the Gestapo officer changed his mind.

"You are no longer free," he screamed.

"Lie down on your stomachs, hold your hands behind you, and do not look up." By this time, the prisoners were so drained that they simply did what they were told.

After what seemed like a long time, Cecylia got up to look. All she saw were small mounds of SS helmets, insignias, belt buckles, and empty wallets torn and tossed. Gestapo identification papers, ripped into tiny scraps, were blowing about with the snowflakes in the wind.

44.

It took Tyszka six days to walk to Czestochowa, which, by the time he got there, was already fitted with the first trappings of a refugee camp. It was confirmed to him what he had already perceived, that the war was over. In what was to be the first and only clear evidence of Cecylia's whereabouts, he was told by a friendly Russian administrator that she was on a list of those who had been diverted to Nordhausen.

He calculated that Cecylia would not have arrived in Nordhausen before the fighting stopped. It was difficult for him to think about her being forced to march into Germany. Worse, though, were the possibilities that she was alone, abandoned somewhere along the way. He did not want to think about it. Instead, he thought about the day he illustrated her at Auschwitz. It was how he liked to imagine her.

Tyszka felt lost. He did not know where or how to start the search. If he journeyed too far, he would have to leave his father without reliable help. He had left him for a few days at a time in the past, but never longer. It made little difference now that they did not have a telephone, as most of the lines were down.

His mother once told him a story about the time when he was three years old and wandered away from the house into the woods, and how they had found him the next day lying fast asleep under a tree. He was so confused today that he wanted to go into the woods outside Czestochowa and fall asleep again. And when he would finally open his eyes, a radiant Cecylia would be there.

He must do something, anything. Yet he knew that, with his needy father at home, perhaps alone, he could not get lost in an entanglement of useless journeys. By now, he knew that most of the living Jews from Auschwitz-Birkenau were either wandering about trying to get back home while eluding the Russians, or were being herded into refugee camps managed by one or another of the allies. And so it would be difficult to locate her.

He had, too, always admired Cecylia's independence and knew that she would try to get back home on her own, that she would resist being trapped in a refugee camp.

Caught in the tug between continuing his search and going back home made Tyszka a dizzy dog chasing its tail. Although he heard that some of the displaced Jews were being treated like pariahs, he decided to go back to Oswiecim as quickly as possible, even though Cecylia might be wandering about in danger. He was told, too, that some of the returning Jews were being beaten and killed in Warsaw by Poles who had stolen their homes.

For weeks he waited in Oswiecim, taking care of his father, watching out for Cecylia's mother. There was, of course, the satisfaction that the Germans were gone. Yet, the villagers knew they were always in peril from the garrison of marauding Russian soldiers camped along the nearby Vistula.

Life did not improve as much as it simply went on. Baby Bazyli, held safe by his parents' love, was growing, though not yet flourishing.

Whenever any of the Jews displaced from Oswiecim found their way back to the village, Tyszka would seek them out for information about his lost love. In a quiet way, she seemed to have disappeared, as no one knew anything about her.

He refused, though, to accept that their love could be extinguished. Finding Cecylia began to take on a life greater than two people being in love. By nature, he embraced a world he could see and touch, a world whose form and meaning he tried to depict with his art. Favored at birth by images and symbols that grew in his spirit, and nurtured by parents sensitive to the possibilities of love, he refused to give up the dream that he would be with her again.

Waiting for a love beating fast in the spirit to show up in the body was beginning, though, to undo Tyszka. Until one afternoon on his way back to bed in the room where he had spent so many wonderful hours talking with his beloved, he became flushed with the need to do something, anything, about his grief.

He decided to leave his father again and travel to Krakow where, he heard, some of the displaced inmates from Birkenau had gone. Again, he left food for his father while arranging with the timid Mrs. Brydinski to come by when she could.

The journey on his bicycle south to Krakow took Tyszka nine days. He could have made it in less, but after three days of cycling on nearly deserted side-roads, he came upon a small group of Russian soldiers sitting in the middle of a dirt road. He pretended not to notice them, hoping he could just glide by on one side.

"You are driving on the wrong side of the road," an older soldier shouted. Tyszka felt his heart thumping faster.

"I am sorry," he said, hoping an apology would be enough for the unshaven soldier. It was not. A sudden burst of gunfire splattered dirt around the wheels of Tyszka's bike.

"Get off! Come here!" the man ordered. Tyszka's thoughts were not of Cecylia. *Could it be that I have survived Hoss and be killed now by an ordinary soldier?*

"Are you a German?" he was asked. The derisive laughter of the younger soldiers told him that his life hung in the balance.

"I am Polish," he answered while scanning for an escape route. His focus was distracted by the slow motion of someone dressed in white, about fifty yards away in the woods. *Probably a woman,* he thought, because of the feminine way her arms flapped up and down like butterfly wings. At a pace slower than jogging, she moved like a hunchback from tree to tree, no doubt trying to avoid being detected.

"Show us identification now," the leader ordered as the rest of the men began to stand and point their rifles at Tyszka.

"I have none to show. I have come from Auschwitz," he answered.

"You don't look like the ones we saw there. And if you were, so what?"

The tension was as icy as the patches of snow along the road.

"Are you a Jew?" the interrogation continued.

Though he was tempted to lie, he no longer knew what was an advantage.

"I am not a Jew," he answered.

"What is your work before Auschwitz?"

"I sketch faces," he answered curtly, worn down now by the game of cat and mouse.

"So, you are not a German or a Jew. You have taken all the fun out of today."

Suddenly, Tyszka found himself high-stepping to avoid bullets spitting again around his feet. The firing sequence seemed rehearsed, as if the group had done this before to others.

"Run," they shouted at him, as they continued to fire at his feet. For the next minute, Tyszka knew the fear of death and was, in fact, closer to it than the day Hoss stuck the Luger into his stomach. As he ran, he felt like a man trying to avoid raindrops in a storm.

Once he got behind the safety of one of the large pine trees about forty yards away, the drunken band of soldiers seemed to have lost its lust for fun. Another drink of vodka while sitting in the sun to wait for the next victim seemed more inviting.

Tyszka stayed behind the tree, frozen by fear, catching his breath while waiting to make a run to the next tree. He spotted the woman in white again as she ran south. He tried to catch up to her so that he might ask her if she knew anything about a woman named Cecylia Brydinski.

Such was his desperation.

In trying to get back to Oswiecim, Cecylia kept off the roads. It had gotten around quickly that they were dangerous places, especially for a woman traveling alone. She decided to walk in the woods on the edges of the back roads. In this way, she would not get lost, and she would have the protection of the woods.

Every now and then on the journey home, she had to take a chance by practically creeping to a farmer's door to beg for food. She made certain always to do this during the day. The night belonged to predators, and she might be mistaken for one of them and shot.

As it was, she had to be careful even during the day. Fears engendered in the aftermath of war sometimes vent in unexpected ways. People of good will, forced for years to live in fear, might react badly to the unexpected knock on the door. A pointed shotgun, a scream, a lecture. Cecylia could never be certain who might answer the door. Or what fierce dog, trained to protect its master, might leap at her throat.

Wild dogs were a particular menace, as they, too, ran in the woods. She was approached one day by a pack of ten. As they surrounded her, she screamed so loud and with such ferocity that they ran from her. They looked back several times to make sure she hadn't followed them. She felt as if she had burned out her vocal chords.

It was during this leg of her journey that she witnessed a frightening scene one day. A man on a bike was stopped by a band of Russian soldiers. She was in the woods, but not deep enough for comfort. Trying to put distance between her and the confrontation, she continued to creep from tree to tree, catching just a glimpse of what was happening. There was shouting and then staccato gunfire that echoed crisply through the cold woods. She saw a man running toward her, running for his life.

As she hid behind one of the tall trees, she expected to see him struck down by any one of the dozens of shots. The man, now fully in her view, also hid behind a tree. He was covering his head with both hands and standing as straight as he could in an attempt to conceal his whole body. Soon, the firing stopped, and he began to run toward her. As she trusted no one in the woods, Cecylia put as much distance between her and the man as she could. Besides, she had lost her voice. It was not long before he was out of sight.

When he finally made it to Krakow, he decided to go to the cathedral Marjacki, miraculously intact. He could still pray to his God, as he did not know what it was to feel totally abandoned by Him or by hope.

The wonder of the basilica, so contrary to the distorted forms of the world around him, practically made Tyszka numb. Its designed beauty was a contradiction to the bombed buildings, huge craters, hungry people, and disheveled women desperate for their children. Contrary to the uplifting trappings of the high church, everything else was sad.

He walked slowly to the main altar before turning right into pews engulfed by shadows. Every time he talked to God lately, he began to sweat. Today was the same. He waited for a few minutes for the sweating to subside before saying, "I am here, God. I hope you are, too. If you have gone away, please come back.

"I am leaving now. And I am mad at you. It is as if you are playing this little game of 'guess what.' I ask questions, you do not give answers. You have given intelligence to me. You give me a special gift with the charcoal pencil. Yet, I do not understand these gifts. Sometimes I think they make things worse."

The accumulated sadnesses suddenly knotted tight in Tyszka's stomach, and quivered for a way out. And then he screamed. A scream so loud and high that it touched the vaulted ceiling of the basilica like the peal of a loud bell, before bouncing around the archways and up from the floor again to the ceiling.

"Where is my Cecylia?" he howled a primitive sadness that produced a frenzy of echoes so that the frightened worshippers fleeing the church could hear only the bits and pieces of his plaintive roar. "Where …where…where…my …my…Cecylia…Cecylia …Cecylia," rang throughout the great expanses of the church before Tyszka got up and also ran out the side door.

He looked everywhere in Krakow that he thought it was smart to look—the semi-disorganized police department, and the remnants of schools where lost people were beginning to place notices, hoping to be found. And where others tacked family photos, hoping to find the lost. In bombed-out synagogues. In the square.

Nothing.

45.

A swirl of feelings spun in Tyszka's heart. He had put all his hopes into finding Cecylia in this city. Lying in the woods at night along the way, he pictured her here, in a torn dress, perhaps helping abandoned children to find their way again. In the dream, he would be told to go to a street called Krolewska to a small wooden building. He would know it because it was newly painted white. She would be there. Just open the door, and she would be there, playing with the children. Always waiting for him.

It was as if the spirit of life was gone from his chest, his heart. He breathed breaths, but they no longer had vitality. When Cecylia was with him, the sun was always shining, and everything else he could see, touch, feel, brush against, hear, know—everything else was in the background of her beauty.

We each have one chance to meet that rare person, he thought. Even though the yellow haze of depression was beginning to come over him, the realization that Cecylia and he loved each other made his heart hop in his chest, so that, at least for the moment, the joy of possibility spurred him to make the journey back to Oswiecim. He was grateful that his father would be waiting there.

Being faithful to his gift by standing up to Hoss left him feeling strong, and while his heart was a nest of contradictions, the depth of his intuition was growing. He began to sense the intentions of people he met along the roads while searching for Cecylia. Gradations of good and evil were more apparent, as was an expanding awareness about the easy progression of one to the other. He knew by now that Baby Bazily, born whole, pure and clean, could become Commandant Hoss. And while Mietek Kerner had cut his world today with the hard carbon of hatred, he could tomorrow be the diamond clean and pure.

Even on his own best days of generosity, Tyszka knew that he was always full of selfishness, and that if he did not nurture the goodness of his birth, he could fall to evil with the ease of gravity.

Something seemed different about Oswiecim on the day he arrived back there. When he came out of the woods north of the little village for the walk home, he sensed a softer cooing of the mourning doves that strutted along the dirt roads at this time of year, as if to announce the coming of spring. They stood together by the score, their eyes shut, their voices hushed and at peace with weeping, as if trying to give him the space to cry.

Suddenly, he knew. He was free. To cry and to laugh. To run to Cecylia's house. It was as if the molecules of air rippling through, over and around Oswiecim were trying to tell him what they had known since yesterday. That Cecylia was home.

Tyszka's legs and feet kicked dust and ashes about as he ran, trying to keep pace with thoughts of seeing her. It was the last few moments of waiting, again, for his parents to get out of bed on Christmas morning. He was running through the mist that separated yesterday from today.

When he finally came upon the front door of her house, he did not know what to do. He was so filled with the doubts of the past few months that he wondered if she would remember him.

He knocked hard on the door. Would it ever open? Finally, there stood Cecylia in front of him. He waited for the mist to evaporate. He was afraid to look at her, afraid that she, too, might disappear in the knitting of time.

"Oh, my Tyszka," she whispered. "Hold me, please hold me."

They held tightly, as if pressing hard against their dreams of being together again, knowing the bliss that is known only to those who have wandered through hell before being rescued.

Standing still in the doorway, Tyszka said, "I would like you to do something for me, Cecylia"

"What is it?" she said.

"I would like you to breathe into my mouth. I have heard it said that if someone breathes into your mouth that their spirit will live in you always and forever."

A tiny smile of understanding came into her face as she remembered the day, perhaps it was in another lifetime, when he first asked her to be a part of him. With the perfect sensing mechanism of his gift, Tyszka knew she was happy.

Cecylia closed her eyes before turning her head upwards. Then she took a breath that filled her with the spirit of their little village, of things past and of things to come, before breathing herself into Tyszka's soul.

RUDOLF HOSS WAS HANGED AT AUSCHWITZ ON

APRIL 16, 1947.

Photo by Tom Phelan

GERARD BROOKER is the author of *A Quiet Conversation, Even Whispers Can Be Heard,* and A *Gathering of Doves.* His essays have appeared in many newspapers and magazines. He grew up in New York City, and lives with his wife in Bethel, Connecticut.

To contact the author please write to:
teacher_jerry@hotmail.com